THE BLACK ANGEL

Christi Walsh

ISBN: 1508719632
ISBN 13: 9781508719632
Library of Congress Control Number: 2015903712
CreateSpace Independent Publishing Platform
North Charleston, South Carolina

1

She'd definitely taken a wrong turn somewhere. Abby wished she had brought someone on this minivacation with her. She could have asked her neighbor, but Ashley and her husband, Jeff, seemed be going through something right now, and Abby hadn't wanted to rock the boat. She had asked Ashley if there was something she could do to help, but Ashley had told her that she had done quite enough. Abby wanted to know what she meant by that but was met with stony silence. So she had left it alone and hadn't pushed. She'd give them time to work it out; then Abby would talk to her.

It was just as well, because Abby had wanted some alone time without any distractions. She was a kindergarten teacher in Portland, Oregon. She loved her kids, but even a kindergarten teacher needed some downtime. They were on their winter break, so this was going to be a nice, quiet trip.

The mother of one of her students had told her about the San Juan Islands in the state of Washington. "It's not that long a drive, and it's beautiful," she had told Abby.

Abby had left Portland later than she'd meant to and driven to Anacortes, Washington, where she had just barely caught the last ferry to Friday Harbor. When Abby had looked up information about the small town, the San Juan website had said its population was just a little over 2,800 people. It offered whale watching, shopping, hiking, and other outdoor activities to explore. Abby enjoyed all those things, so it had sounded like just the right spot to unwind.

She had decided to rent a small house rather than stay in a local hotel and had found one on the Internet. The property-management company had told her it was secluded and private. It was nestled in pine trees with a view of the Pacific Ocean. It had looked perfect to Abby.

When she had driven off the ferry, she went through Friday Harbor. There was really only one main street with shops and restaurants. There were a few trinket shops that looked interesting to her. All the shops were closed, but Abby knew she could explore another day.

The property management had given her directions, but it looked as if she'd taken a wrong turn somewhere. It was dark, and she couldn't see all the street signs. There had been houses scattered around randomly at first, but now Abby didn't see lights anywhere. She was in the middle of nowhere. There were just lots and lots of pine trees. She was sure it was probably beautiful, but at the moment they just looked scary.

The road didn't seem to be in good condition either. It was narrow and bumpy and was starting to look more like a dirt road than the paved one she'd started on. She had just decided to turn around when her car started making a funny noise.

No, no, not now!

"Please, please don't do this to me," she begged out loud. She had just gotten the car out of the shop that day, and that was the reason she had gotten a late start.

The car was starting to slow down. Abby tried giving it more gas, but it kept on sputtering. "Damn it," she muttered as she pulled over to the side of the road. That's all she needed, a car hitting her while she was sitting in the middle of the road, although Abby didn't think it was likely. She hadn't seen a car in quite a while.

Once she was pulled over, she put the car in park. She didn't know if she should turn it off or not. *What if I can't get it started again?* she thought.

Did it matter anyway? She couldn't drive it now. She decided to leave the car running just because it made her feel better; she reached for her bag and grabbed her phone.

"Damn, damn, damn." She had no service. Abby looked around, trying to decide what to do. It was very dark and quiet, and Abby felt alone in the world. She tried to find any kind of light to follow, but it was useless. She was starting to feel a little panicky. She had no idea where she was or how far the nearest anything was. Just then, her car sputtered one last time and died.

Knowing she didn't have any choice, she got out and shut the door. She looked around. Everything was quiet except the wind blowing in the trees. Abby shivered from the stiff breeze blowing and decided she was officially creeped out.

This felt like one of those horror shows she had seen on TV. There was probably a man with a chain saw looking back at her from the trees. "Stop it, Abby, you're not helping yourself."

Trying to shake her nerves loose, she opened her car door again. She grabbed her coat and bag and reached for the flashlight in her glove compartment. *At least I had one in there,* she thought. She mentally patted herself on the back.

She grabbed her keys from the ignition and locked her doors. She turned the flashlight on and pointed it down the road. She was turning to walk back the way she had come when she heard a noise coming from the other direction.

Abby stopped and listened. She smiled. It was a car. She could hear it clearly now. *Thank you, God.* She headed that way. She had only gone a few feet when she realized she couldn't hear the car anymore. *If I just keep walking that way, I should run into it, right?* Maybe there was a house nearby, and they had stopped. She had no idea what was ahead, but she figured right now it was her best option.

She started walking again, trying to ignore all the different noises she could hear in the trees. She kept telling herself there wasn't a man holding a chain saw out there. She was pretty sure there was some kind of animal, though. *Maybe a bear,* she thought, *and I am his dinner. Are there bears on the island?*

She heard a twig snap. She swung her flashlight toward the trees, her heart pounding. Abby tried to see in the darkness beyond her light. She didn't see anything moving except the damn trees. Abby stayed frozen in place, swinging her flashlight back and forth, trying to keep her fear at bay.

Once she decided nothing was going to jump out at her, she started walking again. It was more like a jog than a walk. She couldn't wait until she got cell service again. The first person she was going to call was the mechanic who had fixed her car. Unladylike, Abby snorted. The mechanic who had pretended to fix her car.

Abby had just come around a bend in the road when she saw the car. She let out a breath of relief, thanking the stars above; she wasn't going to be eaten by a bear after all. When she was closer, she realized there were two cars parked on the side of the road.

She ran the rest of the way, her feet pounding on the hard surface. When she got to the first parked car, she looked inside. There wasn't anybody there. She went to the next car. Same thing. She looked around. They had to be there somewhere.

Abby was looking around in all directions when she heard talking. The voices sounded like they were coming from the trees. She couldn't hear what they were saying, but they seemed to be arguing. *Great, now what am I supposed to do?*

Abby knew one thing: she wasn't going to walk in the dark anymore by herself. She'd rather deal with whoever was arguing. Then she realized she would have to go into the scary trees. She took a deep breath and headed in the direction of the raised voices.

Luckily, they weren't too far. She was close enough now to see two men, standing close together. One of the men was waving his arms around as if he was trying to explain something. The other man just stood there, not saying anything. Abby thought this was a strange place to have a conversation. *Why did they go into the trees to talk?* she wondered. *Why not just stay by their cars?*

Abby was starting to get a bad feeling. Something held her back from making herself known, so she stayed hidden in the trees. The man doing all the talking was saying something about a shipment. He was tall and slim. The other man still hadn't said anything. He wasn't as tall but much thicker built, and he was bald. He looked like he could be a body builder, and he gave Abby the creeps.

"It's not my fault. Hank said he knew these people and that they were solid."

Abby continued to watch, staying hidden in the trees.

The other man finally spoke. "I don't care what Hank say. It's you who responsible." He was talking so quietly Abby had to strain to hear what he was saying, but she could tell he had some kind of accent. Abby couldn't be sure, but she thought it was Russian. "And that means it's you who pay."

The man had moved so quickly it took Abby a moment to realize what happened because there was no sound. The man had taken a gun out of his coat and shot the other one.

Abby gasped and took a step back. She must have made a noise because the man with the gun turned to where she was standing. Abby quickly crouched down to her knees. She covered her mouth with her hand, trying to quiet her breathing. Her heart was hammering inside her chest.

She peeked through an opening in the trees. The man was still standing there, looking her way.

"Whoever you are, you might as well come out. I know you there."

Abby didn't move. No way was she stepping out of these trees, because Abby knew in her heart he wouldn't think twice about killing her. She'd seen his face and could identify him.

"Come on out. I not going to hurt you," the man said with his thick accent. He had no panic in his voice. Apparently killing a man was an everyday occurrence for him. So killing her wasn't going to matter either.

Abby started to breathe harder when the man started walking to where she was hiding. She knew she couldn't stay here any longer. She was going to have to make a run for it. But where could she go? She didn't have any idea where she was.

Abby watched the man getting closer. She had to go now! Mustering up all the courage she had, Abby stood and immediately started running back toward the road. She heard the man chuckle behind her. The man actually chuckled, like he was playing a game.

He's crazy.

Abby could hear running feet behind her. Her heart was beating so hard she thought it was going to come out of her chest. She was running, stumbling on the uneven ground, trees slapping her. She felt a few of them cut her face.

She could see the road. Then what? Where was she going to go? She had just stepped on the road when she heard the man behind her.

"Where you going to go?" His accent seemed thicker than before.

Abby didn't turn to see how close he was. She ran across the road and into the trees. She thought the trees would give her the best cover. She didn't slow but charged her way through. She could hear him on the road now. Abby figured she had a couple of minutes on him. If she could just get far enough ahead of him, she could stop and catch her breath.

Five minutes later Abby had to stop. She couldn't breathe, and she had a stitch in her side. She hid behind a tree and peeked around it. She couldn't see anything in the dark, so she listened instead, but her breathing was so loud it was hard to hear anything else. Abby looked in every direction, trying to see something that would give her a clue where she was, but all she saw was trees.

When her breathing was once again under control, she took a few more minutes to listen. Abby whipped around when she heard a twig snap to the right of her. He was even closer now. Not wasting any time, she took off to the left and deeper into the trees.

Abby could hear him behind her. "If you stop right now, I promise I be easy on you," he said in that accent she was beginning to hate. She knew she wasn't going to be able to outrun him. Her only chance was to hide. She took a few precious moments to look around. Then she spotted a clump of trees to her left, and she could see a small opening between the trees. If she could wiggle herself inside, he just might pass her. If she couldn't see, he couldn't see.

She was heading for the clump of trees when Abby remembered what she was wearing. She looked down at her white coat. No wonder he could follow her; she was wearing a beacon. She quickly took her coat off and tossed it as far as she could in the opposite direction from her hiding spot. She thanked her lucky stars she had chosen to wear a black turtleneck sweater underneath. But even with the thick sweater, she felt the chill on her skin.

Not wasting any more time, she hurried over to her hiding spot. The trees had fallen at some point and had stacked on top of each other to provide a nice little hole for her to crawl into. Praying there weren't any creepy-crawlies inside, she squeezed through the opening, lay on her back, and waited.

Abby was shivering, and she didn't know if it was from the cold or fear. Before long, she heard footsteps. He had stopped running and was walking very slowly. It was so quiet she could hear his breathing. Abby covered her mouth so he wouldn't hear hers.

Abby couldn't see him, but she heard steps crunch on the ground just a few feet from where she was hiding. Her stomach twisted with tension. If he saw her, there was no way she was getting away from him. His steps sounded closer. He was so close now that Abby could see the back of his head. He was just standing there looking around. If he turned around, he would be able to see her.

Very quietly, she started moving farther under the tree. Abby had to swallow a scream when she felt something crawling on her leg. She ignored the stinging sensation, and with her heart in her throat, she inched a little closer to the tree.

The man still hadn't moved. Abby didn't make a sound. She was sure he was trying to listen for her, so she stopped and held her breath. She heard him move and almost cried out when he sat on the tree she was hiding under. "I know you out there. I be honest. I won't hurt you." Abby didn't believe him. He would kill her just like he did the other man.

She waited, barely breathing. It seemed like an eternity, but it was only moments when the man stood. He slowly moved away from where Abby was hiding. "I find you, soon or later." She heard him moving away, so she peeked between the trees. He was standing where she had thrown her coat. He bent down and picked it up, looking around again. Abby ducked back down once again. *Please, please just leave!* Abby let out her breath when she heard footsteps walking away from where she was hiding.

She stayed hidden for another twenty minutes even though her muscles were starting to protest. She wanted to make sure he was long gone. She started to feel the chill creeping into her bones. It had been raining earlier, and her clothes were wet from the damp ground, but she was grateful that it had stopped.

Abby listened again for any noise that might make her think that the man was still around, but she didn't hear anything except the wind in the trees. She slowly inched her way up, just enough to peer over the fallen tree. She looked around and decided that he was indeed gone. She stood up and climbed out of her hiding spot, trying to work out the kinks in her body.

She felt exposed out in the open again, and she knew she couldn't stay there all night. She would freeze to death without her coat. She didn't know which direction to go, but she definitely wasn't going the way she had come. With one last look around, Abby started out, hoping she was heading toward civilization.

She didn't think the man was around, but she still tried to keep as quiet as she could. She hadn't gone very far when she felt the first drop land on her face. *Great, just what I needed.* She kept moving in the same direction, hoping it would lead to somewhere. She couldn't see very far in front of her. Abby wasn't sure when she had lost her flashlight, but she wished she had it now.

She stumbled again over some fallen branches. She was going to break an ankle if she wasn't careful. The rain was coming down hard now, and she was drenched within minutes. Her hair was flat to her head, and her clothes clung to her like a second skin. The chill from before was mild compared to what she felt right now. Abby didn't think she would ever be warm again.

Abby had no idea how long she had been walking. She was tired and soaked head to toe. She was about ready to take a break when a tree branch smacked her in the face. *Damn! That hurts.* She was pushing it back and out of the way when she saw a light ahead. Abby pushed her bangs out of her eyes, trying to get a better look. It was still far away, but she was sure it was a house. *Thank God.*

Abby started moving faster, wanting to get to the house. *There must be somebody there, right? Or why would a light be on?*

Even if there wasn't anybody there, it was shelter. She'd break in if she had to. She wasn't sure what the school would think of her breaking and entering, but at this point she didn't care.

When Abby was closer, she stopped to see if she could get a better look. *Yes! It's a house.* And it looked like there were several lights on. Somebody had to be there. Abby started moving again, but in her excitement, she didn't see the tree stump coming out of the ground. She fell hard and hit her head on a rock. *Damn, I was so close,* she thought before blackness took over.

2

Paine had always liked the rain. It was a good thing, too, since he lived in Portland. It had more rainy days than sunny ones, but he loved it there.

He loved being a cop, too, but the last couple of years had been hard ones. He was now divorced from his wife of five years. That was still a tough pill for Paine to swallow. He looked at his divorce as a failure, and he knew he couldn't really blame his ex either. He had never been around. He had picked up a stalking case a few years ago, and it had taken over his life. Not that he regretted taking on the case, but he did regret that it had cost him his marriage, even though deep down, he knew it was over before that.

It had been a hard case. A woman had caught the attention of a stalker, and Paine and three of his best detectives had been assigned to protect her. The stalker had attacked Kate several times and killed a man who had made a pass at her in a bar. It had taken over two years to catch the guy, so they had all formed a close friendship with Kate. In the end they did bring him in, but it had cost several women their lives.

Kate now lived in Wyoming with her new husband, Jack. Paine still talked to her at least once a week. He promised her he would come for a visit in a couple of months.

Now he was on the San Juan Islands to enjoy a little R & R.

It rained a lot here, too. He had been coming to the islands for most of his life. His mother grew up here, so it was like a second home to him.

Paine was just lighting a fire when someone started pounding on his door. He looked at his watch. It was pretty late to have a visitor. He grabbed his gun off the table and headed for the front door, keeping the gun hidden behind his back.

He barely had the door open when someone came barging through it. He briefly registered that it was a woman. A woman who was soaked through.

"Shut the door!" the woman demanded urgently. Paine just stood there looking at her. Even with her hair plastered to her head, she was quite pretty. She looked back at him with almond-shaped green eyes, and Paine could see she was terrified.

"Shut the damn door!" she practically yelled.

"Look, lady. I don't know who you are or why you're even here, but you don't get to give orders without explaining—"

Before Paine could finish, the woman rushed passed him and slammed the door shut. She moved over to the front window and was pulling the curtain aside to look outside. Paine watched her without saying anything. She was tall for a woman. She was at least five nine. He also couldn't help notice how nicely proportioned she was—from the back, anyway.

She turned suddenly and looked at him. "Do you have a phone?" she asked. It wasn't quite a demand, but it was close. That's when he noticed the cut above her brow.

"I have a cell phone, but getting cell phone service here is always a fifty-fifty shot," he said, smiling. She didn't return the smile.

"You're hurt," Paine said.

She started pacing, not saying anything.

"Do you mind telling me what's going on?" Paine asked a little impatiently.

She kept pacing, not answering him. He was getting tired of waiting for her to explain, so he stepped in front of her.

She seemed surprised, as if she had forgotten he was there. Paine had to admit that hurt his ego a little. "Do you want to tell me why you were out in the rain in the middle of the night?"

She looked up at him. "I…" Then she burst into tears.

Paine was momentarily stunned. Not knowing what to do, he put his gun in the back of his pants and tried to reach for her, but she was backing away from him.

"Why do you have a gun?" she asked her eyes wide.

Well, he thought, *the good news is she's stopped crying.* But now she was looking at him as if he were going to attack her or something.

Sighing, he put his hands back down by his sides. "My name's Mark Paine. I'm a cop from Portland. I'm just here on vacation."

"Can I see your badge?" she asked, her voice trembling.

Paine pulled his badge from his coat pocket. He could feel her eyes watching him. He handed it to her.

She took it from him and examined it. She took her time, too, but it gave him time to really look at her. Her hair was dark, but it was hard to tell how dark with it being wet. It looked like it had been in some kind of braid, but most of it had come out. She had high cheekbones, and her lips her full. She was really quite a looker, but Paine's patience was about at its last straw. He told himself be patient, because something obviously had happened to her.

She handed the badge back to him without saying anything.

"Now will you please tell me what the hell is going on? Or even your name?"

Paine watched her as she moved over to the couch. He tried to keep his gaze from wandering over her, but she had a very nice backside. If he didn't stop ogling her, he was probably going to scare her.

"My name is Abby Turner," she began, looking at him. "I was trying to find a house I rented for the week when my car died."

Paine saw her shivering. "Wait. Let me get you a blanket or something to warm you up." Paine went to his room and grabbed a quilt off the bed. He went back to the living room and tried to wrap it around her shoulders, but she leaned away from him, giving him that scared look again.

"Abby, I'm not going to hurt you. I just want to get you warm." Paine waited. After a small hesitation, she nodded. He gently wrapped the quilt around her, and then he stood and walked over to the fireplace. He thought giving her some space would make her feel more comfortable. Then maybe she would tell him what the hell was going on.

He watched her closely. She was just sitting there staring into space. Besides being soaked, she had tiny cuts across her face, and a large bump was starting to form on her brow. "Can you tell me what happened to you now?" he asked gently.

She blinked a couple of times and looked up at him. It was really starting to annoy him that she always seemed to forget he was there. He saw her take a breath. "I—"

The glass window behind her head shattered.

"Get down!" Paine yelled as he dropped to the ground, pulling his gun out. He looked at Abby still sitting there. She hadn't moved. He started crawling over to her. "Damn it, Abby, get down."

She still didn't move. Paine was rushing to get to her when another bullet whizzed by his head. He ducked lower. When he finally reached Abby, he pulled her down roughly by her arm. She didn't make a sound. More bullets went flying over their heads. Paine covered Abby with his body. *What the hell is this woman involved in? And why did she bring it to my doorstep?*

Knowing they couldn't stay huddled on the floor forever, Paine looked around to see what his options were. If they could crawl to his bedroom without getting their heads shot off, they could go out the door that led to the backyard. Paine had no idea how many were out there, but he didn't see any other way. It was a chance they would have to take. He turned back to look at Abby. She seemed to be frozen with fear, and she still hadn't said anything.

"We're going to slowly make our way over to that door over there." Paine pointed to his bedroom door. When he got no response, he looked at her again. "Abby," he said louder. Still nothing. Maybe the bump on her head was worse than he'd thought. He gently shook her. "Abby, look at me."

She slowly turned her head to look at him.

Paine's heart twisted a little. He didn't think she was hurt, but she *was* scared out of her mind.

"Abby, we have to move. We can't stay here."

She was looking at him with that same blank stare as before.

He took her shoulders and shook her a little harder. "Listen, lady," Paine said harshly. "Either you get your butt moving, or I swear to God I'll leave you here and let you take care of this yourself."

Paine knew he would never leave her, but she didn't know that. It seemed to work because now she was scowling at him. She didn't say anything, but she turned and started crawling over to the door.

That's when Paine noticed how quiet it was. The bullets had stopped. It seemed Abby noticed, too. They both stopped. Paine turned back to the window, listening. He heard footsteps outside moving slowly.

"I only want girl," a voice said outside the window. It was a man with some kind of accent. "You give me girl, I let you live."

Paine turned back to look at Abby, and his gut clenched. She was looking at him as if he were going to turn her over to this maniac. Then he got angry. *What kind of man does she think I am, anyway?*

"Move it," Paine said angrily. He knew his anger was off base because, after all, he just threatened to leave her there.

Abby started moving toward the door with Paine following behind her. When they reached it, Paine motioned for her to stop. He looked back toward the window just to make sure the man wasn't coming through it. Paine didn't have to worry about the window, because he noticed the door handle starting to turn. He jumped up, grabbing Abby with him. He opened his bedroom door and shoved her through it, locking it behind him. He felt a sting on his left shoulder. He ignored it, grabbed Abby's hand, and ran over to the slider on the other side of the room. He quickly unlocked it and tried to slide the door open. It was stuck. *Damn it.* This door had been giving him trouble all week. He was going to fix it yesterday but went fishing instead.

Paine put both hands on the handle and pulled. He felt a sharp pain rip through his shoulder. The bedroom door rattled. He was pulling on the door again when he felt Abby come up and put her hands over his. Together they pulled. Just when they got the slider open, the bedroom door crashed open. He heard the woman scream. Paine didn't look. He grabbed her hand and ran out into the night.

Abby never thought she would be so happy to be out in the cold again. When she heard the door crashing open, she had just wanted out. Now she was running with a man who was a stranger to her, but for some reason she trusted him. She didn't know if it was because he had just risked his life for her, or if it was the look she saw on his face when she didn't know if he was going to turn her over to the crazy man. He had seemed angry. And for a moment she had seen disgust on his face. Whichever one it was, she knew in her heart she could trust him. *I hope.*

Abby didn't know where they were going, but he seemed to know, and this time she was just grateful she wasn't out there by herself. He wasn't saying anything, which was fine with her; she didn't think she could answer anyway. She was using all of her energy just to breathe.

He stopped suddenly. Abby wasn't prepared and ran into his back. She lost some more precious air. *Who knew a back could be so hard?*

He turned to steady her. "Are you okay?"

All Abby could do was nod. She bent over with her hand on her side trying to catch her breath. Abby had always considered herself to be in good shape, but now she might have to rethink that.

Once she had some air in her lungs, she straightened and looked up at this stranger who was risking his life to help her. He was very tall. She usually didn't have to look up to anybody, but her head only came to his shoulders. That would have to make him six three or four. *Stupid thing to think about now, Abby, considering you have a crazy man chasing you.* She saw him looking around. "Don't you know where you're going, Mark?" Abby didn't mean for it sound so bitchy, but she was scared.

He scowled. "Call me Paine, and if you would like to lead, then by all means, you show me the way." He moved his arm gesturing for her to move ahead.

Abby scowled back at him. "You don't have to be so nasty. It just seemed like you knew where you were going before."

She heard him sigh. "I know where we are, but I'm not sure where we should go."

That didn't make Abby feel any better. "What do you mean?" Abby asked, annoyed. "We go where there's help. Or a phone that works. Or to a house where it's warm."

Okay, she might have gone too far. He was clearly angry now.

"Because lady," he said through clenched teeth. "We are too far from town to get police help. I already told you cell phone service here is shitty, and third, do you really want to get some innocent people involved with whatever you got yourself involved in?" He said the last part as if it were her fault she was in this mess.

Abby started to fire back her reply when she saw Paine stiffen. "What is it?"

Paine didn't answer her. He put his finger to his lips, giving her the be-quiet sign. Abby looked around but didn't see anyone. They had run for what seemed like forever to Abby. Surely the crazy man hadn't caught up with them already.

It was Abby's turn to stiffen at Paine's next words. "There's more than one."

Abby was shaking her head. "That can't be," she whispered. "I only saw one. Well, two, if you count the man who got shot."

Paine moved so quickly that Abby let out a little scream. Next thing she knew Paine was covering her mouth and nose with his hand. Abby couldn't breathe. She began to struggle, not knowing what was wrong with him. No matter how much she twisted and turned, she couldn't get loose.

"Abby, stop fighting me," Paine said, breathing heavily.

Abby wasn't listening. She'd had all about she could handle for one night. First the crazy man, and now this one was trying to suffocate her.

"Abby, stop it," he whispered harshly.

Abby felt his hold on her loosen. This was her chance. She punched her elbow into his stomach and then stomped on his foot. It gave her a small satisfaction to hear a grunt of pain come from him. She twisted again and found herself free. Not hesitating, she took off in an unknown direction.

She had only gotten a couple of yards when she was suddenly knocked to the ground, flat on her stomach. It felt like a ton of bricks had landed on her, and her breath left her again.

"Damn it, Abby. Why are you fighting me? I'm trying to help you."

Abby felt the ton of bricks lift off her. She didn't move because she was still fighting for air.

Abby almost screamed again when Paine whispered in her ear, "I'm going to turn you over. Please be quiet and don't fight me. We're in serious trouble here." His words started to penetrate Abby's foggy mind. He'd said, "We're in trouble," not "You're in trouble."

Abby felt hands on her upper arms slowly turning her over. Now she was lying on her back looking up at Paine, whose brows were pinched together with concern. "Are you done fighting me now?" he said, still whispering.

Abby nodded, trying to get up. Paine took her hand and elbow and helped her up. Once they were both standing, Abby stepped away from him. This seemed to irritate him because he was giving her the same glare as before. "Look, Abby, I'm not the bad guy here. You landed on my doorstep. Remember?"

Abby pushed her soaked hair out of her eyes. "I'm sorry. I thought you were trying to suffocate me, and I panicked. This night has been the scariest and craziest of my life." She fought back the tears. She was not going to cry in front of him. She'd already lost it once back at his cabin. She had frozen back there when the bullets had started flying. Obviously, she was not good under stressful situations.

She must have sounded pathetic, because the next thing she knew, strong arms were wrapped around her. "It's okay. I thought you were starting to scream. I just wanted you quiet." Paine dropped his arms from her.

"Soon I need to hear what exactly went on with you tonight. But right now we need to get out of here."

Abby felt the chill when his arms left her. It was silly, but she missed those arms. They made her feel warm and safe, which was even sillier, considering that just minutes before, she thought he was trying to choke her.

Paine took her hand, and they were once again running through the black shadows of trees. Abby didn't know when it had started raining again, but both she and Paine were drenched. Living in Portland, Abby was used to rain, but she was never out in it as she had been tonight. Her hands felt numb from the cold, and her teeth were chattering. She tried not to think about how cold she was and instead concentrated on putting one foot in front of the other.

They had been running for a while, and Abby knew she was going to have to stop and catch her breath. If she lived through this night, she was definitely hitting the gym. She was just about to tell Paine she needed a rest when he suddenly stopped, and again she ran into his back. She really wished that he would stop doing that or at least give her some kind of warning. And to top it off, she noticed he wasn't even breathing that hard.

Paine turned to look at her. "There's an empty cabin about two hundred yards ahead."

"Great." Abby said still trying to catch her breath. "Then why did we stop?" Abby hoped she sounded less bitchy this time.

"I want you to stay here while I go check it out."

A terror so strong came over Abby that she started shaking. "No. I want to go with you." Abby hated the way her voice shook, but she couldn't help it. She was scared of being left alone again.

Paine took her shoulders in his hands. "Abby, I'm not deserting you. I want to make sure it's safe before we go in." And then he hugged her. "I'm going to hide you over there under those bushes. I'm not going to let anything happen to you. I promise."

Abby put her arm around Paine and hugged him back. She believed he would keep her safe. This calmed her nerves somewhat. Embarrassed for hugging him, she stepped out of his arms. "I'm sorry I got you into this," Abby said, not able to look at him.

Abby felt his fingers on her chin, lifting it so that she could look at him. She never realized before now how handsome he actually was. He had blue eyes and a strong chin. He reminded Abby of the Marlboro man, except without the mustache.

"I'm not sorry, Abby." Something fleeting came into his eyes, but it was gone before Abby could figure it out. "I was getting bored anyway," he half joked, releasing her.

Really? He was making a joke? She was scared out of her mind, and he was making jokes.

Paine took her hand and led her over to the bushes he was talking about earlier. "I'm not sure about this, Paine," Abby said, eyeing the bushes. "Maybe I should just go with you." She turned to look at him. "You said yourself you thought there was more than one. What if the other one comes?" *And I really don't want to hide in any more bushes.*

"Abby, it's going to be okay."

She watched as Paine started moving the bushes around. She kept watching him as he brought over some fallen tree branches. She'd already seen he was tall, but now she noticed he was also very muscular. Not bodybuilding muscular, but the muscles were in the right places. He was definitely a fine example of a man.

Abby had been so involved in checking him out she hadn't realized he was looking at her. When she looked up at him, he was smiling, knowing exactly what she had been doing. Abby blushed from her head to her toes. She was thankful it was too dark for him to see her pink hue.

"Okay, in you go."

Abby was grateful he didn't comment on it, but his words brought her back to her situation. He wanted her to get into the bushes. She hesitated. She still didn't think this was a good idea. Abby turned to tell him she wasn't going to do it when he suddenly bent his head and kissed her.

Abby was too shocked to do anything except stand there. Then she found herself disappointed when he pulled away. "I won't be gone more than ten minutes. Don't come out until I come get you." He pushed her down into the bushes, and before she knew it, she was lying on the ground, and Paine was gone.

Abby was once again hiding in some trees with the wet ground soaking through her clothes. *Will this night ever end?* She started shivering. If she kept hiding on the wet ground, she was going to catch pneumonia. Trying to forget about the cold, she thought about the kiss they had shared.

Paine was a good-looking guy, and she was attracted to him. What girl wouldn't be? He was also strong and confident. Those were all nice qualities that would attract any girl. She had been attracted to other men before, but Abby felt something else. It was like she was drawn to him. *Maybe it's because he's helping me. That had to be it.* She was a practical girl and just didn't fall for somebody ten minutes after meeting him.

Abby didn't know how much time had passed when she heard a noise. She stopped breathing. It was footsteps. Maybe it was Paine coming back. She waited for him to call her name. The footsteps were closer now. *If it was Paine, wouldn't he have called out by now?* Abby's heart started racing. This was definitely déjà vu. She didn't move a muscle. In her hiding spot she could see a pair of tennis shoes walking toward her.

3

Paine hated to leave Abby, but he needed to check out this cabin to make sure they weren't walking into an ambush. It was an old cabin that hadn't been lived in for years. Some of the windows were broken, and some were just missing. It wasn't much, but it would provide them some kind of shelter.

When Paine reached the clearing where the cabin was, he stopped and looked around. He didn't see movement in any direction. He walked to the edge of the clearing until he could see the back door of the cabin. If somebody were in there, they would expect him to come from the front.

When he was in position, he once again looked around. It looked empty but he still didn't move. Even though he wanted to get back to Abby as quickly as possible, he waited a few precious minutes before he moved toward the cabin.

Paine didn't see any activity from inside the cabin, so he stepped into the clearing and headed for the back door. When he reached it, he turned the handle, not surprised to find it locked. He put his uninjured shoulder to the door and pushed. It gave in after a couple of shoves.

The first thing he noticed was the smell. *Something must have died in here,* he thought. He walked through the kitchen, noticing a dining table pushed into a corner. In the living room, there were old newspapers thrown all around the floor, and dust was everywhere. It looked like nothing had been touched in years.

Just to be sure, he went through the whole cabin. It didn't take long. It was small, with only one bedroom and a small bathroom. Deciding the coast was clear, he went back through the kitchen to go out the back again.

Once he was outside, he looked around for a small stick. When he found one, he leaned it against the back door. It wasn't much of a security system, but it was the best he had right now. Paine looked around once again for any movement. He scanned the edge of the clearing; deciding it was clear, he started for the trees. He had to stop the urge to haul ass back to Abby, but in his experience as a cop, he knew caution was the best way. That didn't stop him from moving a little faster than normal.

There was something about her that drew him to her. Yes, she was pretty. Quite beautiful, actually, but there was something else about her. She was strong and vulnerable at the same time. She was asking for help one minute and then giving him orders the next. He had to smile at that. Whatever the reasons were, he knew she needed his help. Whatever she gotten herself into, he would help her. He just hoped she wasn't some kind of criminal. It would be a shame to have to put her nice little behind in jail.

Paine was almost to the spot where he left Abby when he stopped and listened. He tensed when he heard footsteps to the left of him. They were moving away from him and from the cabin. *That's good,* thought Paine. When the footsteps had faded, he once again started moving to get to Abby.

"Abby? It's Paine." He said when he reached her hiding spot. He waited for her to come out. His heart began racing when there was no movement from inside. He knelt down and started frantically moving the shrubs and sticks away. He knew she was gone before he saw the empty space. "Damn it."

He jumped up, looking around. "Abby," he whispered even though he wanted to scream her name. Paine looked around in all directions. *Why would she leave her hiding spot? Did they find her? How many are out there?* He could swear it was only one set of footsteps he had heard earlier.

Paine looked down and could just make out one set of prints on the ground. They were large, like a man's. Somebody had been standing here. He followed the footprints. They were going in the direction of where he heard them earlier. And there was still only one set of prints. Abby wasn't with him. What if he was carrying her? Paine wasn't a tracker. He couldn't tell by looking at a footprint if they were carrying someone or not.

"Damn it," he swore again. He shouldn't have left her.

Paine started moving toward the trees, hoping he would be able to follow them. It was his only clue. He had only gone a few steps when he heard it. Somebody was moving in the trees behind him. Paine quickly jumped behind a tree and listened. Whoever it was, they weren't very quiet. Then he heard cursing. He let out a breath and smiled. *Abby!* He stepped out from the tree.

"Where the hell did you go?" he asked more harshly than he intended to. Paine couldn't help it. She'd scared the hell out of him.

Abby let out a little scream and whirled around to face him. Paine watched her face go from terror to relief and then to anger. He had to admire her spunk.

"Where the hell did *you* go?" she fired back.

"I told you to stay put and I would come back and get you," Paine said, moving toward her. "Is it so hard to follow simple directions?"

Abby was also moving toward him. "Listen, jackass. If I hadn't moved, I would have been found." When she was close enough to him, she started poking him in the chest with her finger. "Your little hiding spot wasn't such a great hiding spot."

Paine couldn't help but smile. She was beautiful standing there reading him the riot act. It had started to rain again, and her hair was once again plastered to her head.

"You told me you would be right back," she said. "You were gone—"

Paine didn't wait to hear the rest of what she was going to say. He grabbed her and brought her in close to hug her. It felt good to just hold her. He had met this woman only a couple of hours before, but somehow she was already becoming important to him. Paine must have startled her into silence. She wasn't hugging him back, but she wasn't fighting him either.

"God, Abby, you scared me to death," Paine said, pulling her back so he could look at her. "I thought they had found you." Abby stared up at him. He couldn't read her expression. Paine had to fight the urge to grab her again when she stepped out of his arms.

"I'm fine. You were right, though. There are two of them." Abby turned from him and started to move into the trees.

Paine gently touched her arm to turn her around. "How do you know? Did you see both of them?"

"No. This man was wearing jeans and tennis shoes. The man I saw earlier was wearing a suit and tie."

"A partner?" Paine asked.

"How the hell would I know?" Abby said tersely.

Paine really needed to get her story, but the rain was coming down harder now. He could see Abby starting to shake from the cold.

"Come on," he said, grabbing her hand. "Let's get to the cabin and get you warmed up."

4

Abby let Paine lead her out of the trees. She was just too tired to do anything else. She had decided she was caught in some kind of time warp, because this night seemed as if it would never end. When Paine had sneaked up from behind her, she about came out of her skin. She didn't know if her heart could take any more scares. If somebody had asked her if she'd thought this was how she would spend her first night of vacation, she would have laughed and told them that they had some kind of imagination. Abby still couldn't believe that she was living this nightmare, and to top it off, now she needed to pee.

"Um, Paine?" *What kind of name was Paine, anyway?* He stopped walking and turned to face her.

"What's wrong now?"

Abby stiffened at his words. "I'm sorry, but I need to use the restroom," Abby said with as much dignity as she could.

Paine sighed. That just made Abby even angrier. "I'm sorry, but don't you ever have to use the restroom?"

"Relax, Abby. I'm not upset that you have to use the restroom. I'm sorry I didn't think to ask."

"Oh." Now Abby felt ridiculous.

"Pick a tree, Abby." She just looked at him. "In case you haven't noticed, we're not near a restroom."

Abby bristled. "I know we're not near a restroom. I'm waiting for you to go away."

Paine shook his head. "No way, Abby. I'm not leaving you again."

Abby was looking at him as if he had lost his mind. "I'm not going to pee in front of you!"

"Why not?" Paine asked.

"Why not?" Abby practically yelled. "Because, because—"

"Shh, keep your voice down," Paine whispered. "Look, Abby, go behind that tree." Paine said pointing to a large tree a few feet away. "I won't be able to see you, but you're still close in case our friend comes back."

Abby put her hands on her hips. "Can you at least cover your ears?"

Paine blinked at her. "What?"

"Cover your ears. So you can't"—this was so embarrassing—"hear. Okay? So you can't hear." Abby blurted out, not looking at Paine. There, she'd said it. To her annoyance, she heard Paine laughing. "What is so damn funny?" she asked irritably.

"I think you're adorable. That's what." Paine turned away from her. "I'll cover my ears *and* turn my back. Now go." Abby watched to make sure Paine did both the things he said he would and then made a bee-line for the tree. A few minutes later, she came back around from the tree and smiled. Paine still had his back turned and his ears covered. Abby walked over and tapped him on the shoulder.

He turned to look at her. "Better?" he asked.

"Yes, thank you." She smiled.

Paine brushed the back of his hand softly over her cheek. "You're welcome." Abby wanted to press her face against his hand, but fortunately he removed it before she could make a total fool out of herself.

"Let's go. It's not much farther," Paine said, back to business and a little bossy.

Abby was blindly following him, daydreaming about the way he had touched her cheek earlier, and wasn't paying attention to where they were going. She ran into his back when he stopped suddenly. "Oh, sorry," she mumbled.

"You see that cabin in the clearing?" Paine asked, pointing. Abby saw a structure, but she didn't think she would call it a cabin. It had a roof on it, though, and she could get out of this rain. She would hide in an outhouse if it would get her out of the rain. She nodded, not saying anything.

"Once we leave the trees, we're going to run to the back door," Paine was saying. "I don't want you to stop for any reason. You got it?"

Somehow he always made it sound like he was talking to a two-year-old. "Gee, I think so," she said sarcastically. Paine frowned at her but didn't say anything.

They inched a little closer to the clearing. Abby saw Paine looking around, so she did the same. She didn't see anything. Apparently he didn't either, because he turned to look at her. "Ready?"

Abby nodded. She felt him give her hand a squeeze before they were off and running. Abby made sure to keep up with Paine. She didn't want him to think she was some kind of wimp. Her breathing was starting to come in short gasps. She didn't think the cabin was that far away, but with the rain and wind, Abby found herself fighting for breath.

Just when she thought she was on her last breath, they reached the back door of the cabin. Abby bent over, trying to catch her breath. She could feel Paine moving around. Abby lifted her head to watch him. He was removing a stick that was leaning against the door.

He turned to her. "I want you to stay here. I think it's clear, but I want to make sure. I should be back in twenty seconds. No longer. If I'm not, I want you to run back to the trees and hide."

Before Abby could say anything, Paine disappeared through the door. She started counting in her head. *One Mississippi, two Mississippi.* She had barely gotten to seven Mississippi before Paine stood in front of her again.

"It's clear." He held out his hand and waited for her to take it. After a slight hesitation, Abby took Paine's hand. The cabin was small and had some sort of smell to it, but Abby didn't complain. It was dry.

"I know it's not the Ritz, but we're safe here for a little while." Paine let go of her hand to turn a chair upright. "Here, have a seat. I don't want to start a fire, but there are some blankets in the bedroom. I'll be right back."

Exhausted, Abby sat down in the chair. She looked around the small cabin. The kitchen and living room were one "big" room. She could see a door that must lead to the bathroom. She was deciding if she should risk using the bathroom again when she saw Paine come out of another door. Must be the bedroom.

"I want you to take off your clothes and wrap up in this blanket."

Abby stared at him.

He chuckled. "Abby, you can't stay in those wet clothes. We have to get you warm." When Abby didn't move, he sighed. "I promise you—I am a gentleman. You can ask my mother."

Abby was freezing, but did she really want to give up her clothes? "What if that man comes here? I don't want to have to run with just a blanket and my ass hanging out."

"That's why I'm here. To cover your ass," Paine said, smiling.

Abby could see the twinkle in his eyes, but somehow that didn't make her feel any better. Paine reached down and picked her up by the shoulders. "I told you, we're safe for now. They won't find this cabin in the dark." He pushed her toward the bedroom. "Bring them back out here, and we'll spread them out to get them as dry as possible before we have to leave again."

Abby was still hesitant, but the thought of being dry again sounded wonderful, almost enough to risk running with her ass hanging out.

With one last look at Paine, she started toward the bedroom.

"Leave the door open."

That stopped her. She turned to look at him.

"If you shut the door, you won't be able to see. It's dark in there."

Abby looked harder at him. *Was he joking or being serious?* She really couldn't see his face in the dark, so she assumed he was serious.

She turned again and went into the bedroom. Abby was pretty sure she heard Paine laughing. But he was right; she couldn't see anything in here. She stood to the right of the door so he couldn't see her. She had her shirt off and was just getting ready to pull down her pants when she heard something scurrying across the room. Abby screamed and ran out the door and into a hard chest. She landed on her bottom.

"Shit, Abby. What's wrong?" Paine said lifting her up again by her shoulders.

"I heard something in there." She pointed back to the bedroom. "I'm thinking a snake or mouse." Abby looked up at Paine. To her annoyance, he was trying to hold back his laughter. "Look, I don't care if you think that's funny or not. I don't do snakes *or* mice. I've had about all I can take for one night. So you can stand there and laugh all you want," Abby said, her voice getting louder. "I am not going back into that room!" She walked around Paine and headed for the back door.

"Where do you think you're going?"

"Outside. And I don't care if it's raining or not."

"Without your shirt?" Paine asked mischievously.

Abby looked down, and for the first time she realized she was indeed without a shirt, standing there with just her bra on. Could this night get any worse? It was just too much. To Abby's horror, she felt the tears coming. She couldn't stop them. She was trying to prove to Paine she wasn't a wimp, and now she was standing there without a shirt, crying. This was the most ridiculous night of her life. If she weren't the one living it, she would be laughing by now.

Abby felt Paine come up behind her.

"Please just go away," she said. "This is embarrassing enough without you laughing at me." Abby felt the warmth of the blanket being wrapped around her.

"I'm not laughing at you, Abby. I know you've been through something tonight, and I want to hear exactly what it was, but you need to get dry." Paine moved around to face her. "How about I hold this blanket up, and you can take off the rest of your clothes here. That way you won't have to go back into the bedroom."

Abby looked up at him, shivering. Did she trust him enough to take off her clothes in front him? *What a stupid question.* She just ran blindly through the dark woods with him. He could have done any number of things to her, but all he did was protect her all night. Besides, she really didn't want to have to go back in that room.

"I promise I won't look," Paine said teasingly.

Making up her mind, Abby nodded.

Paine took the blanket and held it up in front of her. Not wasting any time, Abby took off her bra and shimmied out of her wet jeans, dropping them to the floor. She left her underwear on. She just couldn't stand to be completely nude. If she did have to run, at least her ass wouldn't be completely hanging out. "Okay, I'm done," Abby said, reaching for the blanket. Paine didn't let go.

"Turn around," he said gently. Abby turned her back and once again felt the warmth of the blanket being wrapped around her along with Paine's arms. Not able to stop herself, Abby leaned back against his chest. He always seemed to make her feel safe.

"You're safe with me, Abby," Paine whispered, as if he could read her mind. "I won't let anything happen to you."

Abby felt him kiss the top of her head. She could stay like this forever. Abby wasn't sure how she got lucky enough to find this man's cabin, but she couldn't help thanking the stars above for leading her to him.

Abby didn't know how long they stood there with Paine just holding her, but too soon she felt him pulling away. Abby had to resist the urge to turn to him and ask him to keep holding her. She already knew she was attracted to this man—a man she just met a couple of hours before. But she was going to stick to the whole hero-worship thing and call it good. Sighing, Abby moved away from him.

She watched Paine as he started for the bedroom. "Where are you going?" Abby hated the panic in her voice. She was sounding like that two-year-old.

"I'll be right back," Paine said over his shoulder.

Abby could hear him moving around in the bedroom. A few minutes later Paine walked out, carrying a single mattress. She watched him carry it to the middle of the room and lay it down. "At least it's better than sitting on the floor," he said, looking at her. "Come over here and sit down." He was back to talking to her like a two-year-old.

He was the only man who could turn her on one minute and make her want to take a swing at him the next. Abby decided not to argue and moved over to the mattress and sat down, trying not to notice the stains that were all over it. Once she was seated, she looked up at Paine. An odd expression was on his face.

"What's the matter?"

"Nothing." Paine shook his head. He started to unbutton his pants.

"What are you doing?" Abby asked anxiously.

"Relax, Abby. I'm wet, too. I also need to get dry." Abby felt ashamed that she hadn't even thought about his discomfort. He didn't seem to be shy about undressing in front of her, and she didn't seem to be shy about watching him. She stared as he unzipped and started pulling his pants down. To Abby's annoyance his shirt hung down to his thighs. She did, however, admire his legs. They were long and muscular. She was still admiring his legs when he pulled his shirt over his head. Abby swallowed. Oh my, the man was built. He looked like he could be a model in a magazine.

She'd seen six-packs in magazines, but that didn't compare to seeing one in person. She always dated reasonably good-looking men, men who even had nice bodies, but those men had nothing on Paine. Abby was starting to move her eyes down lower when she heard Paine clearing his throat. She looked up at him. To her horror, he was grinning. Abby quickly looked away, and she could feel the heat climbing over her face. He just caught her staring at him. Again! Not just staring, but ogling. Then she thought about it and got angry. It wasn't her fault he caught her staring.

"If you don't want me to stare, then you shouldn't undress in front of me."

Paine chuckled. "I don't mind you staring, Abby. In fact, I like it. I just wish we were somewhere else—a different place and a different time. Then I would show you how much I like it."

Abby didn't know what to say or do, because the truth was, she wouldn't mind.

Paine turned to sit down next to her. Abby saw the blood on his shoulder and tried not to gag. Ever since she was a little girl she couldn't stand the sight of blood. She was still trying to prove to Paine that she wasn't a wimp, and she didn't think throwing up would help her case. "Oh my gosh. You're hurt." Abby tried to reach for him, but he shied away.

"It's okay, Abby. It's just a flesh wound." He wrapped his own blanket around him. "Believe me, I've had worse." Once he was seated, he turned to face her. "Now why don't you tell me what happened tonight and how you wound up at my doorstep?"

He might as well have dropped a bucket of cold water over her, because the statement brought Abby back to reality and her situation. She started to shiver again. Paine put his arm around her shoulders. "Remember, Abby, you're safe with me. I will help you, but I need to know what happened."

Nodding, Abby started her story. "My car died, which is annoying because I'd just gotten it out of the shop that morning." She told him about coming upon the two arguing men.

"Do you know what they were arguing about?" Paine asked.

"I'm not sure exactly. It didn't make sense to me, but the man who got shot said something about 'these people are solid.' The next thing I knew, the man with the accent shot him." Abby started rocking back and forth. "I must have a made a noise or something, because he knew I was there. But I stayed hidden. I don't think I could have done anything to stop it, Paine, but I feel like I should have done something."

"Abby, there was nothing you could have done." Paine squeezed her shoulders. "It sounds like you interrupted some deal that had gone bad."

"I left him there. All I could think about was getting away." She cried.

Paine put his hand on her chin and turned her face to look at him. "If you had stayed, you would be dead now. You couldn't have helped that man. His fate was probably sealed a long time ago."

Abby knew Paine was right. Nothing about this night was her fault. She just happened to show up at the wrong time in the wrong place.

Abby realized Paine was still holding her chin. She looked into his eyes and knew he was going to kiss her, and she did nothing to stop him. She watched as he slowly lowered his head. Her heart started to pound in her chest. He was looking into her eyes, and then he lowered his eyes to her mouth. When he was just a breath away, Abby closed her eyes.

The first touch of his lips on hers was like heaven. This kiss was different than the first time he kissed her. This time he was gentle and made Abby feel as if she were a delicate flower.

Abby liked the feeling, but she wanted more and needed more. She reached up and took his face in both her hands and kissed him back wantonly. Abby was surprised at her boldness, but it didn't stop her. She pushed Paine to his back and was on top of him. Her blanket had fallen to the ground, but she didn't notice. All she could think about was Paine and kissing him and how much she wanted him. Abby felt Paine's arousal against her stomach. She felt his hands on her back, caressing her everywhere. It was as if he couldn't get enough of her, either.

Abby started to move her hand down to caress him when she felt his hand cover hers, stopping her. Abby groaned in protest. She tried to move her hand again, but it wouldn't budge. She lifted her head to look at Paine.

"Abby, honey, if I don't stop now, I won't be able to."

"Why do we need to stop?" Abby couldn't believe that just came out of her mouth. *What am I doing?* She was about to have sex with a perfect stranger. Well, he wasn't a complete stranger, but she had only known him for a short time. Mortified, Abby jumped up and off Paine. She stood, looking down at him, breathing hard. He probably thought she always had sex with men she didn't know. Paine, however, wasn't looking at her face. He was looking lower. Abby looked down and suddenly realized she didn't have her blanket. She quickly covered herself with her arms.

"Abby, please don't be embarrassed."

"I'm not embarrassed." Abby said looking around for the blanket. *Where the hell is it?* Spying it a couple feet away, she quickly grabbed it and wrapped herself in it. Just when she thought this night couldn't get any worse, she'd made a complete fool out of herself. Abby didn't know which was worse, the crazy man trying to kill her or embarrassing herself by jumping Paine's bones.

"Abby."

"It's okay, Paine. I must have let the night get to me. You know, being almost killed and everything." She tried to shrug it off.

Abby jumped when she felt Paine come up behind her. She hadn't even realized he had gotten up. "Abby, I think you're beautiful and sexy as hell. But we both know you would have regretted it later."

Abby didn't say anything but knew he was right. She would have regretted it. It wasn't her style to jump into bed without having some kind of feelings for the person. It scared her that she was so willing to with Paine because she thought the feelings were there. It would probably scare him if she said that out loud. "You're right, Paine. Let's just forget it."

Abby started to move away when Paine grabbed her hand. "I'm not going to forget it, Abby. Believe me I want it as much as or more than you do." Surprised, Abby turned back to look at him. "That's right, Abby. I want you. And I'm not going to forget it, because when we're out of this mess tonight, I will be coming back to finish what we started."

Abby didn't say anything. She just smiled at him and walked away.

5

Paine let her go. *Damn, what just happened?* Had he actually stopped Abby before they went any farther? What was wrong with him? Since his divorce, he had gone out on many dates. Even had a serious relationship with one woman but soon realized it wasn't what he had wanted. There was something about Abby that was different. He wanted it to be different with her. He hadn't wanted her to regret making love with him. He knew she was attracted to him, but what he didn't know was how much. He didn't want to be a one-night stand but knew in his heart that Abby wasn't a one-night-stand kind of girl. He couldn't think about it anymore. He had to get her to safety. She'd obviously walked into something dangerous tonight. In order to help Abby, he needed to find out what that was, but he couldn't do that until she was safe.

He looked around the room for her. She sat huddled in a corner. She looked so sad and vulnerable he wanted to go over there and take her in his arms, but he knew that wasn't a good idea.

"Abby, you should try to get some sleep. You look exhausted."

She didn't say anything. Paine walked over to her and held out his hand for her to take. At first he didn't think she was going to, but after a few seconds Abby took it.

Paine helped her up and started to lead her back to the bed. "Come back over to the mattress." Abby's step faltered. "It's okay, Abby. You need to sleep. And so do I," he said, pulling her again toward the bed. "I can't keep an eye on you when you're way over there."

When they reached the mattress Paine sat down, bringing Abby down with him. He lay down. Abby didn't follow. "Come on, Abby. I just want to hold you. Please just let me hold you." He hoped he didn't sound too pathetic. He really just needed to touch her and make sure she was okay. Abby was looking at him, but Paine couldn't tell what she was thinking. After a moment she lay next to him with her back against his chest. He put his arm over her waist, inching a little closer to her. Paine could feel the tension in her body. He didn't say anything, letting her get used to him.

"Tell me something about yourself," he said.

"Like what?"

"What did you say your last name was?"

"Turner."

"So where do you live when you're not here being chased by a crazy man, Abby Turner?" Paine asked, hoping to help her relax.

"I live in Portland also." Paine could hear the smile in her voice.

"And what do you do in Portland?"

"I'm a kindergarten teacher," she said proudly.

"Wow, you really must like a challenge."

Abby laughed. "It is a challenge. It's a good challenge, though. It's fun watching new ideas come to light for them. It's almost like a new world coming into shape right before your eyes."

"It sounds like you really enjoy it."

"I do." She paused. "Well, most days I do. As you said, there are some challenges." Abby moved a little closer to him. Paine tried to ignore how she felt against him. Her soft curves and her bottom pressed against him. He needed to think of something else before he embarrassed himself. Fortunately, Abby did it for him.

"So you're a cop?" she asked.

"Yep, for twelve years now."

"Did you always want to be a cop?"

"I'm going to tell you a secret, a secret that you can't share with anyone, especially my fellow detectives."

Abby turned slightly so she could see his face. "Really? This sounds interesting."

Paine looked down into her smiling green eyes. "I wanted to be a dancer."

Abby started laughing.

"Hey, what's so funny?" Paine asked, pretending to be hurt. "You can't see me as a dancer?"

"No...yes, I'm sorry. What I mean is that you're so big and tall. I just thought dancers were a little more—"

"Graceful?" asked Paine, smiling now. "My dance teacher would agree with you. Very quickly I realized that I probably couldn't make a living as a dancer."

"So why a cop?" Abby asked, yawning and turning away from him. Paine realized she was almost asleep.

"I decided if I couldn't dance, then maybe I could help people."

"I'm glad you're a cop, Paine. And a dancing one," Abby said, her voice fading.

A few minutes later he felt her body relax as the exhaustion took over. He lay there and listened to her breathing. Paine knew he had a problem when it came to her. He hadn't been this attracted to a woman in a long time. At least since his wife, but even this felt different than it had with her. The question was what he was going to do about it. *What do I want to do about it?* Paine didn't know, but he did know Abby was in trouble, and he would do everything in his power to help her. Or die trying. In the morning he was going to get her to safety and then call his detectives to help him. Paine didn't care if it was out of his jurisdiction or not. He was going to get to the bottom of this mess. When he felt he had a plan in place, he let his own exhaustion take over.

Paine suddenly sat up. He didn't think he had been asleep for that long. If he had to guess, he would say only a couple of hours. What woke him? He looked down at Abby, still sleeping. Then he heard it again. Footsteps. And they were outside the cabin. Damn, how did they find the cabin? It was so isolated. Nobody should have found them. He must have tracked them somehow.

Paine bent down to Abby, shaking her gently. "Abby, honey, wake up," he said quietly. She groaned in protest. Paine almost covered her mouth to keep her quiet, but after the last time, he didn't think that would be a good idea. "Abby, you need to wake up. There's somebody outside." He whispered a little louder. What he had said must have penetrated, because she quickly sat up.

"Is it him?" she asked in a frightened voice.

"That would be my guess. We need to get out of here," Paine said urgently, grabbing for his clothes. "I don't think he knows we're here yet."

Paine saw Abby reaching for her own clothes, thinking she was going to give him hell if she had to make a run for it with her ass hanging out. Paine had to smile at the thought.

"What the hell is so funny?" Abby whispered angrily.

Paine didn't answer, but instead he reached for his shoes and gun. "Hurry up. I think he's almost to the back door. Which means we're going out the front." Once he had his clothes and shoes on, Paine stood and stalked quietly over to the only window in the room. He looked out, not seeing anyone at first. Then a shadow passed over the window. Someone was walking toward it. Paine jumped away from the window with his back pressed against the wall.

"Abby," he whispered urgently, "stay down and don't move." Abby continued to put her clothes on. "Abby, stop!"

Abby stopped what she was doing and looked over at Paine. He motioned for her to get under the blanket. He pointed to the window. Abby's eyes widened when she realized what Paine meant. Not hesitating, she dived under the blanket and didn't move.

A few seconds later Paine heard someone wiping the window to see inside. His heart was pounding.

Should he make his move now? What if Abby some-how got caught in the crossfire? He couldn't risk it. He decided the best move was to get out of there without being seen.

Paine had no idea how long he stood there, but eventually he heard the footsteps move away and start around the cabin. He moved quickly over to Abby hiding under the blanket. "Abby, let's go." He yanked the blanket off her. He grabbed her arms to help her up, happy to see she had her clothes on. Paine started for the front door.

Abby pulled free of his hold. "I need my shoes."

Paine went back for her shoes and once again grabbed her arm. "Come on, you'll have to wait to put them on. We have to leave now!"

They both stopped when they heard a noise at the back door. Paine wanted to shoot at the man who had been trying to kill Abby, but instead he turned back to the front door, twisting the knob. It turned in his hand, and luckily it was quiet. Once he had the door open, he pushed Abby through it. He shut the door quietly behind him. "Okay, Abby." Paine looked at her frightened face. It tugged at his heartstrings. "Same as last time. Just run for the trees and don't stop for anything."

When Paine saw her nod, he grabbed her hand and started for the safety of the trees. He figured they only had a few minutes to reach them before the man fig-ured out that they had been there and came looking for them. With every step they took, Paine expected the bullets to start flying again. He said a silent thank you when they reached the trees without incident. Once he felt they were out of sight, he stopped and ducked behind a rock, bringing Abby with him.

"Here put your shoes on now." Paine handed them to her. He looked back at the cabin. The front door opened, and the man walked out, looking around. Paine couldn't see him clearly enough to see his face. He was taller than Paine, but he figured he probably stilled outweighed him by fifty pounds. The man didn't seem to be in any rush or panic to find them, and it made him wonder why.

Paine could feel Abby moving next to him. He turned to look at her, noticing she now had her shoes on. "You did good, honey," Paine said, smiling. Abby gave a slight smile back. He turned back to look at the cabin. The man was gone. Paine looked around, not seeing him anywhere.

"Now what?" Abby asked anxiously.

Paine turned so he could rest his back on the rock. "We keep moving until we find help. I thought we would be able to wait it out in the cabin, but obviously that plan has changed." He looked at the cabin once more. "It will be light soon. I think there are a couple of houses about two or three miles from here. Someone should have a phone we can use, and then we can get some help."

"I thought you didn't want to get anyone else involved with this," Abby whispered.

"I think we're close enough to town and civilization that he wouldn't risk it." Paine stood and held out his hand for Abby to take. She took it this time without any hesitation. "As soon as I can get to a phone, I'm calling for backup."

"You mean the police?" Abby asked.

"Well, them, too, but I meant my detectives back in Portland." Paine thought this was bigger than local police could handle. As much as he hated to do it, they might even have to call in the FBI. Something was going on in this little town, and he figured he was going to need the help.

6

A bby didn't think she had ever been more tired or cold or even miserable than she was right then. It seemed as if it had been hours since they left the cabin, but in actuality it had probably been only been an hour or so. Her right foot was hurting. She was pretty sure it was bleeding from stepping on something sharp, like a rock or pebble. Every step felt like a needle going through her foot. She wasn't going to complain, though. Paine had saved her life more times than she could count that night. She didn't want to have to tell him she was hurt, too. She was already a big enough pain as it was.

Abby could see the sun just starting to rise on the horizon. This long horrible night was almost over. They would get to a phone and get some help. They would catch the guy, and it would all be over. What about Paine? Would she see him again? Would he disappear as fast as he appeared? Her heart was saddened by that thought. She felt they had connected somehow, or maybe it was just the whole protection thing again. Somehow Abby didn't think so. She was attracted to Paine. *Hell, I almost had sex with him.* If he hadn't stopped them, she would have. Abby didn't want to think about that fiasco. She could feel the warmth on her face again, thinking about the way she acted. Abby was not usually the aggressor in her relationships, but Paine seemed to bring it out in her.

Abby had been so lost in her own thoughts she didn't realize Paine had stopped until she ran into his back. "Oh, sorry." She really needed to stop doing that.

Paine turned to steady her. "There's a house just ahead of us."

Abby peeked around Paine to see. "Well, let's go, then." She tried to move around him, but he stopped her.

"It's still early. We don't want to scare these people."

"That sounds perfect. We scare them, and they call the police. We're saved."

Paine chuckled. "Yes, that would be perfect. Except I don't know these people. What if they have a guard dog they let loose on us? Or worse, they have a gun?"

Abby couldn't hold back her frustration. "What do you suggest then? Call and make an appointment?"

Paine scowled at her. "No, but after surviving the night, I don't want to get shot by some jackass because he doesn't know how to use a gun."

Abby felt foolish. "I'm sorry, Paine," she said, lowering her head. "It's just we're so close."

Paine tipped her chin up. "I know, honey." Abby liked the way he called her honey. "I think we should wait just a couple more hours, and then we'll go knock on their door."

Abby groaned. *Suck it up, Abby; it's just a few more hours.* At least it had stopped raining. She nodded, not saying anything else.

She watched Paine as he looked around them. "Come on. There's some nice soft pine needles over there just calling our names." Abby followed Paine over to the spot he was talking about. It did look soft, but she was pretty sure it was not as soft as a nice warm bed.

Paine sat down first and leaned against a tree. Abby sat down next to him. She felt his hands on her shoulders pulling her back. "Lean against me, Abby. It'll keep us both warm." She didn't argue. She leaned back on Paine's chest, and his arms went around her. She turned so she could rest her cheek on his chest. "This feels nice." *Oops, did I just say that out loud?* "I mean, you're right, it is warmer."

She could feel Paine's laugh rumble through his chest. "It does feel nice, Abby." She could feel Paine looking at her, but she didn't look up at him. "Remember what I told you before, Abby? We are going to finish what we started in that cabin."

Abby swallowed; she couldn't think of anything to say to that.

"Now try to sleep," Paine said.

Yeah, right! How was she supposed to go to sleep? He had just informed her that they were going to make love in the near future. Not that Abby was protesting. She wanted it to happen, but she felt a little out of her league here. Not because Paine was good-looking or built like a Greek sculpture, but because she didn't understand her feelings toward him. Soon they would be out of this mess, and then she could reevaluate them. Was she truly attracted to him, or to the man who saved her life? To her surprise, Abby felt her eyelids getting heavier. Her last thought before drifting off was wondering when she had shaved her legs last.

Later Abby woke to someone stroking her hair. It was nice. It made her feel cherished and protected. "I just realized that I haven't said thank you for everything you did for me last night," Abby said, not moving.

"That sounds like something you say when you're getting ready to say good-bye. You're not trying to get rid of me are you, Abby?"

She sat up and turned to look at Paine. "I didn't mean it like that. I just wanted to thank you before the police or whoever you're going to call got here." She leaned in and kissed him.

It was only supposed to be a quick peck, but Paine put his hand behind her head and deepened the kiss. He devoured her mouth. He slipped his tongue inside her mouth and explored.

Abby moved to get closer. Before she knew what was happening Paine had her on her back, entwining their legs and kissing her senseless. He moved from her mouth to her jaw and down to her neck. Abby felt goose bumps pop out on her arms.

"Abby, I don't know what you're doing to me."

She didn't answer but started to do her own exploring. She started with his back and moved down to his buttocks. This man was too sexy for his own good. Abby felt the cool breeze on her neck when Paine lifted his head to look at her. "I don't want to say good-bye, Abby."

She stopped her exploring. "What are you saying?" she asked, her heart pounding.

"I'm saying that when this is all over, I want to be with you. I want to take you out on a date. I want to take you dancing." He smiled. "What do you think about that?" His smile disappeared, and he was watching her carefully.

Abby realized he was worried. She felt a feeling of power and something else come over her. She didn't want to call it love—maybe a strong liking to love. This gorgeous man was nervous because he didn't know if she wanted to be with him.

Abby smiled mischievously. "Are you sure you're a good dancer? I mean, a girl has to have standards, after all—" Paine had his mouth on hers before she could finish, but she was okay with that. As far as she was concerned, he could kiss her all day.

Abby was just starting her exploring again when Paine lifted his head.

"I'm sorry, honey."

"I know. We have to stop," Abby said, trying to get up.

Paine held her down, looking at her. "You are the most beautiful, strongest, and bravest woman I know. I just wanted you to know that." He lifted himself off her and stepped away.

Abby was stunned. What was she supposed to say to that? Thank you?

"Come on, honey. Let's go get rescued."

* * *

As it turned out, the house belonged to a couple in their eighties with no dogs or guns. When Paine and Abby knocked on the door, they took one look at Abby and quickly ushered them into the house. Paine just shrugged when Abby gave him a dirty look. He didn't regret waiting, though. It gave him a few more hours to be with her. It was probably a selfish move on his part, but he didn't want to give her up just yet.

The couple brought them into a small kitchen at the back of the house. The house was just as old as they were, or even older, but it had been well taken care of. The kitchen, though small, was homey and welcoming. The cabinets had been painted white, and the countertops were a pale-blue laminate. There were yellow sunflowers painted randomly throughout the room. A dining table sat in the middle of it.

"We appreciate you letting us barge in like this," Paine said to the older couple. "My name's Paine, and this is Abby."

Abby smiled at the couple but didn't say anything.

"This poor girl looks like she's about ready to fall down," the woman said, helping Abby into a chair at the table. "And what happened to your head, dear? Did you fall?"

"Oh I'm fine, really. It's just a bump," Abby said, dismissing it.

"I'm George, and this is my wife, Agnes." The man sat down at the table with them. "I've got to tell you, son, we were a little surprised to have visitors this early."

Agnes came over and gave Paine and Abby each a cup of coffee. "You're lucky George didn't grab his gun. He could have shot you."

They all turned to Abby when she choked on her coffee. "Goodness, dear, are you all right?" Agnes patted Abby on the back.

"I'm fine. Sorry. It just went down the wrong pipe," Abby said, not looking at Paine.

Paine laughed. "It's okay, Agnes. She's probably eating some crow right now."

"Boy, what are you talking about?" George gave a Paine a confused look.

"It's nothing, George. Do you have a phone I could borrow?"

"Of course," George said, still looking confused. "Whom do you need to call?"

"The police."

"The police?" Agnes asked, worried.

"We had a little bit of trouble last night. I want to report it."

"What kind of trouble?" George asked, looking excited. "Should I get my gun?"

Paine laughed. "No, it's all right, George." Paine reached into his back pocket and pulled out his badge. "I'm a cop from Portland, and I think the local police should know what happened last night."

Paine looked at Abby and saw her confused look. He shook his head at her.

"Well, do tell, boy, what happened?" George asked, getting up to get the cordless phone off the wall.

"Abby and I were out walking when we came upon what looked like a drug deal. We didn't stick around long enough to be sure, but in our haste we got lost." Paine looked sheepishly at George. "We had no cell service, so we just kept walking until we came upon your house."

"You poor dears," Agnes said with sympathy.

George handed the phone to Paine. "You can call the sheriff, but I wouldn't expect a whole lot help from him."

"Why do you say that, George?" Paine asked.

"Because that boy couldn't find a fly on a donkey's ass."

"George!" Agnes scolded.

"You know it's true, Agnes." George waved his hand, dismissing her scolding.

"What do you mean, George?" Paine asked.

"The only way that boy got to be sheriff is because he has a rich daddy. Everybody in this town thinks he can part water, but I'm telling you, son, there's something off with that man. Nobody knows how he made his money or where he came from, but he's rich, so everyone just accepts him." George paused. "And his son."

Paine turned to look at Abby. "I think I'll call Ben, Jake, and Bill first."

"Your detective friends?" Abby asked.

Paine nodded. "I'll feel better with them covering my back before I talk to the sheriff."

"But won't it take them most of the day to get here?" Abby asked, frowning.

"They can catch a flight to Seattle and then rent a car from there. That should cut off some of their time."

"Do you think that's a good idea?" Abby asked, looking pointedly at Agnes and George and then back to Paine.

Paine looked at the older couple. Was he putting these kind people at risk by waiting? Should they go and wait for his colleagues somewhere else? The decision, however, was taken out of his hands.

"You can wait here for your friends," George said.

"That's right. Abby, you look like you could use a nice warm shower," Agnes said, helping her out of her seat.

"Oh, I don't—" Abby started.

"Now, dear, don't argue. You take a shower, and I'll fix us all some breakfast. Come on. I'll show you where everything is."

Paine watched Agnes hustle Abby out of the room. He smiled and winked at her when she looked helplessly over her shoulder at him. He didn't want to have her out of his sight, but he felt that they were safe here for a little while. *Yeah, right. Just like I thought at the cabin.* He ignored the thought and instead tried to concentrate on what George was saying.

"Now, son, why don't you tell me what's really going on?"

Startled, Paine looked at George. "What do you mean?"

"Son, I've been around long enough to know what bullshit sounds like."

Paine laughed. "I meant no disrespect. I just didn't want to worry you or your wife."

"I can tell you, son, that my wife knows bullshit, too, probably even better than me, but she would never turn away somebody needing help." George got up to refill their coffee. "So let's hear what has you and your lady friend hiding in my house."

"Thank you, George," Paine said quietly, humbled that there were still decent people out there willing to help strangers.

"Think nothing of it, son. Now let's hear it. And more important, will I get to use my gun?"

7

bby couldn't get a word in with Agnes showing her where everything was. "I'll get you some towels out of the hallway." Agnes hurried out of the room. Abby looked around the bathroom. It was also small. A toilet, a pedestal sink, and a tub were lined up in a row. The room was wallpapered in pink roses. It wasn't Abby's style, but in this house, it was pretty.

"Here are your towels, dear," Agnes said, handing them to Abby. "I'll wait outside while you undress, and then I can wash and dry your clothes for you."

Abby protested. "Please, Agnes, don't go to any trouble. It's kind enough of you to let us wait here for Paine's friends."

"Don't be silly, dear. It's no trouble. This is the most excitement we've had in a long time."

Abby laughed. "Well, I'm glad, then." Abby started to say something and then stopped.

"What's wrong, dear?" Agnes asked, concerned.

"I hate to ask, but I think I hurt my foot earlier, and I'm going to need some ointment and bandages."

"Oh, dear," Agnes exclaimed. "Why didn't you say something earlier?" Before Abby could respond, Agnes was heading for the door. "I'll be right back." Abby decided she must have misjudged the ages of George and Agnes. They moved liked a couple who were in their fifties, not eighties.

Abby sat on the toilet and took off her left shoe first and then was starting on the right foot when there was a knock on the door. "Come in, Agnes."

The door opened, and Paine walked in carrying a first-aid kit. "Agnes said you had hurt your foot."

"It's nothing, Paine. I must have stepped on something when I was running barefoot."

Paine bent down on his knees in front of Abby. "Which foot?"

"The right one." A lump formed in Abby's throat when Paine gently picked up her right foot and started to take off her shoe.

"Why didn't you tell me you were hurt?" Paine scowled.

"What could we have done about it?" Abby fired back. "Call a paramedic?" She regretted the words as soon as they came out. "I'm sorry, Paine. I'm not usually this cranky."

"It's okay, honey. I didn't mean to come off cranky either," Paine said, smiling. "I was just worried when Agnes told me you were hurt."

Abby tried to pull her foot from Paine's grasp. "Really, Paine, it's nothing. I can take care of it." Before she could stop him, he had her shoe off, and Abby couldn't stop the gasp that escaped her.

"Damn it, Abby. Your sock is covered in blood."

Abby felt tears coming. "I'm sure it's fine," she choked out.

Paine looked up at her. "Abby, honey, please don't cry." He started to reach for her.

"Don't, Paine." She scooted away from him. "I told you it's fine." Abby was fighting back the tears. She didn't want to lose it with Paine here. "Just go. I can take care of it myself."

"Abby, I know you can take care of it yourself, but I need to see for myself how bad it is. It's my fault you were hurt."

She frowned at him. "What are you talking about? How is this your fault?"

"I made you run without your shoes."

"You made me?" Abby asked angrily. "As I recall, we were running for our lives. You saved me, Paine. Again." She punched him in the arm. "So stop feeling guilty and fix my damn foot."

Before Abby realized what was happening, Paine was kissing her. He had both hands on her face, kissing her like he couldn't get enough of her. She could feel his tongue demanding to be let in. She opened her mouth for him. Abby started to wrap her arms around him when he broke the kiss. "You have to stop doing that," Abby said, punching him again in the arm and then putting her hand on her swollen lips.

"What?" Paine asked. "Kissing you?"

"No. Kissing me and then stopping. It's enough to drive a girl crazy."

Paine laughed. "Honey, when we make love, it's going to be in a soft bed without distractions, and where I can go nice and slow."

Abby gulped. "Okay."

"At least I didn't make you run with your ass hanging out." Paine smiled up at her. "Now let me look at your foot."

Abby had forgotten about her foot when Paine started kissing her. She wanted Paine, and it scared her how much. It seemed as though he wanted her just as much. He had already told her he wanted to keep seeing her. Abby decided she would stop worrying about what all that meant and just play it out. She tried to ignore the little voice in her head that was telling her to watch out for her heart, but she was afraid that it was already too late for that.

"I'm sorry, honey, but this going to hurt like hell. The sock is stuck to your foot."

Abby looked down at her foot. "I hope I don't throw up all over you."

Paine looked up at her in alarm. "Why would you do that?"

Abby chuckled. "Because I don't do blood. I can't stand the sight of blood."

"Maybe you shouldn't look, then."

"It's okay Paine. Just do it." She watched as Paine slowly started to remove her sock. Abby gagged but held it together. She tried to hold in her hisses, but Paine was right. It hurt like hell.

Paine looked up at her. "It looks like there's something stuck in your foot." He waited for her to look at him. "I'm going to pull the sock off the rest of the way, but I'm afraid it might take whatever is in your foot with it." Abby nodded not saying anything. "Ready?" Paine asked.

"Ready," Abby said, holding her breath.

Abby cried out when Paine took the sock off. Her foot felt as if it were on fire. "Shh, honey, it's okay. I'm done." Paine was holding her, wiping her tears. She didn't even realize she was crying. "I'm sorry I hurt you."

Abby leaned away from him and blew her nose. "I keep telling you, it's not your fault." She looked down at her foot. "Paine, I'm bleeding all over Agnes's floor." She was hoping not to throw up all over the place.

Paine didn't move. "I know. I'll take care of it. I just wanted to make sure you were all right." Abby knew for sure now that her heart was almost lost. It still scared her, but not as much now that she had admitted it to herself.

"You really are just a big softy, aren't you?" Abby said through tears.

Paine bent down to take care of her foot. "Just when it comes to you, honey."

Paine worked on her foot for the next few minutes in silence, which was okay with Abby. She didn't want to talk either. She wouldn't know what to say, anyway. They had only met last night, but somehow it seemed longer than that. They had been through so much already, trying to stay alive. Abby hoped her adventure was over. She and Paine could start a new adventure of their own, one that didn't include some crazy man trying to kill her.

"Okay, honey, I think that's it," Paine said, looking up at her. "How are you doing?"

"I'm fine, Paine. Do you know what was in my foot?"

Paine reached for something on the floor. "I think it was some kind of nail." He held it up for her to see. "Have you had a tetanus shot lately?"

Abby laughed. "I'm a kindergarten teacher, remember?" She took the nail from Paine. "We're prepared for anything."

After looking at the nail, Abby tossed it in the garbage can next to her. She looked at the mess on the floor. "I'm going to have to leave money for Agnes and George. I think I ruined their bath mat."

Paine started to clean up the floor. "I don't think they would take it, honey." Once he was done, he stood up, holding the first-aid kit and the bath mat. "I'll take this down to Agnes and see if she can do something with it." He turned to leave and then stopped. "Don't get that wet, by the way."

"Great. How am I supposed to take a shower without getting it wet?"

"I can stay and help you if you want," Paine offered with a straight face.

Abby laughed when she saw the twinkle in his eyes. "Somehow I'll manage."

"My loss then." He started for the door again. "When you're undressed, put your clothes outside the door. Agnes said she would wash them." Then he was gone.

Abby quickly undressed and set her clothes outside the door. Clean clothes sounded wonderful. A shower and food sounded pretty good, too. The thought of food prompted Abby into the shower. It was a little tricky trying not to get her foot wet, but she managed by holding it outside the tub. Abby felt ridiculous, but it worked.

Twenty minutes later she felt like a new woman. She didn't have her clothes back, but Agnes brought her a bathrobe to put on until her clothes were done. She didn't see a blow dryer; so she brushed her hair and left it down to dry. No makeup, either, but she didn't usually wear a lot of makeup anyway. Abby decided it was more important to be dry and warm than wearing makeup. She headed downstairs barefooted, hobbling on her sore foot.

When she entered the kitchen Agnes was busy cooking over the stove, and George was at the table, cleaning a gun.

"You really do have a gun?" she asked, surprised.

"Damn right," George said, holding the gun up and looking down the barrel. "I know how to use it, too. So if that man comes looking for you, I'll be ready."

"How do you know about the man?" Abby was taken aback.

George looked up at her. "Your man told me."

"Oh, he's not—"

"I told him I could handle any trouble that comes knocking at my door."

That worried Abby. "George, if Paine told you about him, then you know how dangerous he is. I don't want you or Agnes to get hurt."

Agnes put her hand on Abby's arm. "Dear, it's okay. George does know how use a gun. And besides"—she turned back to the stove—"he'd be thrilled if he actually got to shoot it."

Abby laughed. "Well, I really hope, George, you won't get to use it."

"One can only hope, dear."

Abby looked around the kitchen. "Where's Paine?"

"Oh I put him in our bathroom to take a shower," Agnes said over her shoulder.

Abby sat down at the table. Whatever Agnes was cooking smelled wonderful. She was starving.

A couple of minutes later Paine walked in. Abby about swallowed her tongue. His hair was still wet from the shower. He was wearing the same jeans, but his shirt was gone, and now he was wearing just a white T-shirt with a V-neck that clung to his torso. She assumed his shirt ended up in the wash also. Abby could see wisps of dark hair peeking out. The man was just too damn gorgeous.

He stopped when he saw Abby sitting at the table. "Hi, honey. Feel better?"

"I…yes, I…" Abby sputtered.

She looked up at Paine. He was smirking. Damn the man. He knew how he affected her. Abby tried to put on her best "whatever" face. Paine chuckled when he came over and kissed her on top of her head. He bent down and whispered in her ear. "You look beautiful." Then he moved to sit in the chair next to her.

Abby hadn't thought she was a blusher, but the last twelve hours had taught her different. She looked at George and Agnes to see if they had noticed, but George was still cleaning his gun, and Agnes was still at the stove.

Paine took Abby's hand into his. "I called the guys. Bill can't come because he's about to close a case, but Jake and Ben will be here sometime late this afternoon." He squeezed her hand and then turned to George. "I hope it's okay if we stay a little longer, George."

"Son, you can stay as long as you like. I'd love to see how this all plays out," George said excitedly.

Paine smiled. "I hope we'll be long gone from here by then." He turned back to Abby. "When Jake and Ben get here, we'll all go to the sheriff's office together. You'll tell him your story—"

"Then I can go home," Abby said, relieved.

She could see there was something else he wanted to tell her. "What is it, Paine?"

"Until they catch this guy, you're still in danger."

"But why?" Abby said anxiously. "Once I describe him to the police, there would be no point coming after me."

Paine put his hand on her arm. "Honey, I know you want this to be over, but this man knows you can ID him. There will be a trial, and you'll have testify against him."

Abby's heart sank. She hadn't thought about a trial. She knew trials could take months and months. Paine was right; she did want this to be over.

She paced, too nervous to sit. "So what does that mean?"

Paine stood up and took her hands in his to stop her. "It means I'll be there for you."

Abby looked up at Paine, tears shining in her eyes. "Why?"

Paine smiled. "I told you I wanted to keep seeing you."

Abby smiled through her tears. "Now who's looking for a challenge?"

He lowered his head and gently kissed her lips. "I wasn't looking for a challenge, but I'm glad I found one."

Abby looked into Paine's eyes. She always thought smoldering eyes were in romance books, but here she was, looking into them right now.

They both heard the discreet cough behind them and broke apart. George and Agnes were sitting at the table, waiting for them to sit down. The gun was gone from the table and was replaced with bacon and eggs and fluffy pancakes. Abby's stomach rumbled.

Paine heard it and laughed. "Come on, honey, sit and eat."

"I guess I am a little hungry," she said, sitting in the chair he pulled out for her.

The next few minutes were busy with filling their plates and taking those first delicious bites. Abby had never tasted pancakes this good before. She ate one and reached for another.

"Agnes, you're going to have to give me this recipe for these pancakes. They're heavenly."

"I could tell you, dear, but then I would have to kill you."

Abby stopped in midreach and looked at Agnes, and then it seemed to dawn on Agnes what she had just said. "Oh dear, I didn't..." Agnes started, clearly flustered. "I mean, I didn't—"

"It's okay," Abby said, laughing. Agnes was still looking distraught, so Abby reached for her hand. "Agnes, really, it's okay. Besides, I could probably get it out of George later."

"Then I'd have to kill him." Agnes's eyes twinkled.

George choked. "We have some mighty feisty women," he said, looking at Paine.

Paine was about to answer when the phone rang. Abby jumped.

"It's probably Jake and Ben. They said they would call with flight information," Paine said, watching George get up to answer the phone. He turned to look at Abby. "You just have to hold on for a couple of hours more."

Abby shook her head, embarrassed. "I'm sorry. I don't mean to be so jumpy."

Paine leaned in so he was just inches away from her. "I think you're entitled to be jumpy, but I promise I'm not going to let anything happen to you." He looked into her eyes. He had those smoldering eyes again.

"Paine." George held out the phone for him to take. With one last leering look and a wink, he stood and took the phone.

Abby turned and looked at Agnes, who was giving her a knowing smile. Abby felt the pink hue again on her face. What would Agnes say if she told her that she'd just met Paine last night? Would she think Abby was foolish? Could two people be so attracted to each other that quickly? Abby looked away without commenting. She couldn't explain it, so she didn't even try.

"That sounds good, Ben," Paine was saying. "I'll see you in about six hours." Then he hung up.

Paine came back over and sat down again. He turned to Abby. "You heard?"

She nodded. "But what do we do until then?"

"If George and Agnes don't mind, I think we should wait it out here," Paine said, looking at each of them.

"Don't be silly, boy. Of course you can wait here," George said.

Agnes stood and started clearing the table. "We wouldn't have it any other way." Abby stood to help Agnes. "Oh no you don't." Agnes took the plate Abby was holding. "You need to get some rest and get off that foot."

Abby started to protest.

"Dear, I've been doing dishes for fifty years. I think I can handle these." She headed for the sink. "I mean it. You and Paine go get some rest. You've had a rough night."

Abby looked to Paine, not knowing what to do. He stood and took Abby's hand.

"Come on, honey. Agnes is right. You need some rest," he said, pulling her toward the door. "I have a feeling that when Ben and Jake get here, things will move fairly quickly."

"Go ahead and take the spare bedroom," Agnes said, going back to the table to clear more dishes. "Oh wait, dear. I forgot to give you your clothes. And Paine, I think your shirt is about done, too."

Agnes disappeared through a door Abby hadn't even noticed before. She assumed it was the laundry room. Agnes returned, holding Abby's clothes and Paine's shirt.

Abby took the clothes. "Thank you, Agnes. Thank you both for taking such good care of us." Abby smiled at them.

"Don't think anything of it," George said, smiling back at her. "As I said before, we appreciate the excitement."

Abby laughed as Paine pulled her out of the kitchen. They went upstairs and headed toward what Abby was assuming was the spare bedroom. "How do you know which is the spare bedroom?" she asked.

"Agnes showed me while you were in the shower."

They passed the bathroom Abby had used earlier and went to the next door. Paine turned the knob and opened the door. They both stood there gaping at the room. Abby thought the bathroom was something to behold, but that room had nothing on this bedroom. The walls were covered in orange roses. And not just the walls—the bed cover and the curtains were also decorated with orange roses. Everywhere you looked were orange roses.

"Colorful, isn't it?" Paine asked.

"I think I'm getting a headache just looking at it." Abby grimaced.

Paine pulled her in the rest of the way and shut the door. He went over to the window and looked out. It reminded Abby why they were here, and the orange roses weren't that important anymore.

"Do you see anything?" she asked anxiously.

Paine turned to look at her. "Everything's fine, Abby." With a last look out the window, he pulled the shade down and started for the bed.

The room wasn't dark, but putting the shade down did help tone down the colorful roses. "What are you doing?" Abby asked, alarmed.

"I'm going to get some rest." Paine lay down on the bed. He looked at her with amusement. "Come on, Abby, we already spent the night together."

"But that was with the rain and the trees and a crazy man after us. This is a…"

"Bed?" Paine finished for her, still amused.

"Yes, a bed." She was angry that he found her so amusing. "A nice soft bed without distractions."

Paine started laughing. "Abby, honey, do you really think I would try to seduce you with George and Agnes downstairs?"

Abby felt foolish again. She had a made huge assumption. This man always made her feel off-kilter, and she didn't know what to do about it.

"Right." Abby sat down on the edge of the bed with her back to Paine. She felt the bed shift.

"But that doesn't mean I don't want to make out a little bit." Paine whispered in her ear. Abby felt goose bumps on her arms again. When she didn't move, Paine got up and sat behind her. "Abby." He stroked her arm. "You're tired. Hell, I'm tired. I'll just hold you and maybe nibble your ear." Abby could hear the smile in his voice. "Let's get some rest."

Abby looked over her shoulder at him. "I'm sorry. It's silly, considering I threw myself at you last night." She paused and thought about it. "And this morning."

Paine pulled her down on the bed and crossed his legs over hers. "I wanted you just as much as you wanted me. I still want you, probably more than I should." He gently moved a piece of hair out of her face and tucked it behind her ear. "We are going to be together, but right now we both need rest."

Paine scooted up so he could lay his head on the pillow. "Come here, Abby."

Abby looked at Paine. He was lying there with his arm outstretched, waiting for her. She moved so she could rest her head on Paine's shoulder, her face near his chest. He wrapped his arms around her.

"I like holding you." Paine said kissing her on top of her head.

"Do you think it's safe for us to sleep?"

"I think we're safe. Close your eyes, Abby."

He didn't have to tell her twice. Abby shut her eyes and was quickly fading.

"And besides, George has his gun."

She smiled, already half-asleep.

8

The man watched the house from the trees. He had tracked the woman for a couple of hours and ended up here. Now he was deciding what to do about it. He looked around. There were no close neighbors, and he could see an older couple sitting at a table in the kitchen. He knew that the woman was in the house, and the man was sure to be close to her. He didn't know who the man helping her was, but he almost respected him for it. It would be a shame to have to kill him.

The Black Angel watched the house for a while to make sure nobody left. He didn't want to kill the old couple either. He would if it was necessary, but right now he was more concerned that they might have called the police.

They call him the Black Angel because he only killed those who deserved it. This woman had caused him more trouble than he expected. She was the most excitement he'd had in a long time. Maybe he could have a little bit of fun with her first for all the trouble she'd caused.

He looked around, trying to find a comfortable hiding place. He saw a rock formation near a large pine tree. Looking at the house to make sure no one was watching, he headed for the hiding spot. He figured it was going to be a long day, and he might as well be comfortable. He was a patient man. He didn't get his reputation by being fast and sloppy. He could wait for days if necessary, but he knew when he got his hands on her, it would have been worth the wait. He settled into his hiding spot and thought about all the ways he could have fun with her.

*   *   *

Paine woke first. He looked around the room at all the orange roses and remembered where he was. He looked at his watch and was surprised to see it was almost four o'clock. Paine couldn't believe he had slept that long.

He felt a weight on his arm and turned to Abby. She was still sound asleep. He watched her sleep. She had dark circles under her eyes, but that didn't take away from her beauty. Her hair was lighter than he thought. When he had walked into that kitchen and seen her sitting there after her shower, her hair free from her braid, her face without makeup, he thought she was the most beautiful woman he'd ever seen. His ex-wife would never have been caught dead out in public without makeup. Abby didn't really have a choice in the matter, but he had a feeling she still didn't wear a lot of it.

Abby stirred in her sleep but didn't wake up. He didn't want to move, but he needed to check on things. He needed to find out how close Ben and Jake were to getting here, and then they needed to form some kind of plan.

He knew Abby was still in danger. Guys like that just didn't give up. Whatever she had walked into felt like a big operation to him. He just didn't know how big yet.

Paine slowly started moving his arm out from under Abby. When he had his arm loose, he carefully slipped off the bed, trying not to disturb her. He went over to the window and pushed the blind aside just enough to peek out. At first he didn't see anything, and just when he decided there was nothing out there, he caught a movement by a tree.

Paine's whole body tensed. He kept watching the spot to make sure he hadn't imagined it. He waited for several minutes without anything else moving. Maybe he hadn't seen anything. He was about to move away when he saw it again. There! He saw what looked like an arm move slightly above a rock.

Damn it, how did he find us?

He would worry about that later, but right now they had to get out of there. He turned to Abby and stopped. She was sitting up and looking at him, terrified.

"He's here, isn't he?"

Paine started moving again. "Get your clothes and shoes on, honey."

Abby jumped off the bed and reached for her clothes. A few minutes later Paine heard her groan. He was beside her immediately. "What's wrong?"

"Nothing, I'm fine." She brushed him away. Paine looked down and realized it must be killing her foot to put her shoe on.

"Abby, I'm sorry. Your foot."

"It's fine, Paine. Just do whatever you need to do, and let's get out of here."

Paine stood and rushed around the bed, grabbing his gun off the nightstand. How could he have been so stupid to think he wouldn't find them here? He'd not only put Abby in danger again, but now he had Agnes and George to worry about.

"You can stop beating yourself up now," he heard Abby say. Paine looked at her. "It's not your fault he found us." Very slowly she walked over to him. "If it weren't for you, I would probably be dead by now." She pushed up on her toes and kissed him softly on the mouth. "But that doesn't mean you can't save me again." Then she turned and headed for the door.

Paine was stunned. *Did she just read my mind, or am I that obvious?*

Abby turned again to look at him. "Are you going to stand there all day, or are we getting out of here?" she said over her shoulder, opening the door.

Coming out of his stupor, Paine followed Abby out the door. He saw her limping, but she didn't complain. His heart flipped a little more.

At the bottom of the stairs they ran into George with gun in hand, looking excited. "I was just coming to get you, son."

Paine tried to not show his concern so he didn't frighten George. "Oh hey, George," he said casually. "What's going on?"

"I don't want to alarm you, but I think there's somebody outside."

Paine sighed. "I know, George. I'm sorry I brought this to your house."

"No need to be sorry, son. I told you before, we would never turn away somebody in need."

Paine didn't know what to say.

"Come on, Son, let's go in the kitchen, get Agnes, and then decide what we're going to do about this son of a bitch." George slapped Paine on the back.

When they all entered the kitchen, both Abby and Paine stopped again and gaped. Agnes stood by the back door, holding a rifle.

Abby started to giggle.

Paine looked at her, frowning, and soon started laughing, too. "This guy has no idea who he's dealing with." He shook his head.

"That's right, son," George said, smiling at his wife. "She's actually a better shot than I am."

Paine walked over to Agnes. "Have you seen anything?"

"He's out there, all right. I think he had to relieve himself," Agnes said. "When you gotta go, you gotta go."

"So what are we going to do about it?" George asked, looking out the window.

Paine was thinking. They weren't going to be able to wait it out here anymore. He needed to call Ben and Jake and make a new rendezvous point.

He turned to George. "George how far is Lime Kiln Lighthouse?"

George thought about it. "I'm not exactly sure, but I'd say ten miles or so."

"Why don't we go into town to the police?" Abby asked nervously. "Even if the sheriff doesn't know what he's doing, he would still protect us."

Paine walked back to Abby. "There's something in my gut, honey, telling me to hold off on the sheriff until we have backup." He bent and kissed her gently on the mouth. Paine didn't think he would ever get tired of kissing her. He lifted his head to look at her. "I'm asking you to trust me."

Abby looked at him, smiled, and then nodded. Paine's heart did another little flip.

Hoping he wasn't making the biggest mistake of his life or Abby's, Paine got on the phone to call Ben and Jake. While he was waiting for them to pick up, he looked over at George and Agnes. They were standing by the door, both of them holding their guns, keeping guard. He looked over at Abby, who had sat down at the table. Except for wringing her hands, she seemed to be keeping it together. Paine had to admire her strength and courage. He didn't think any other woman would have held it together, but he'd already decided that Abby wasn't like any other woman.

Ben's voice interrupted his thoughts. "Paine. What's wrong?"

Paine smiled. His men knew him so well. He wouldn't have called unless there was a problem. "We have a visitor. How far out are you?"

"We're at least another two hours. We left Seattle about forty-five minutes ago."

Two hours felt like a lifetime to Paine. "There's a lighthouse called Lime Kiln. It's on the west side of the island. It's a popular tourist attraction, so it should be easy to find. I think we'll be safe there until you get here."

"Copy that, Paine. We'll see you in a couple of hours. Stay safe." Then Ben hung up. Ben was the no-nonsense guy, short and to the point, whereas Jake was the flirt—a carefree guy. The two of them butted heads once in a while, but they always had each other's backs, and Paine trusted them with his life.

Paine turned to the group. "We have at least two hours before they're here."

"What's the plan, son?" George asked.

"Do you have a car?"

"Of course."

Paine looked out the window. "This guy has to be on foot." He turned back to George. "If we could borrow your car, we could get ahead of him."

Paine watched as George walked over and took a set of keys off a key holder by the door. "It's in the garage," George said, heading that way with Agnes following him. They took their guns with them.

Paine turned to Abby. "You ready?"

"I'm worried about George and Agnes." She stood and limped over to him. "I can't let these people get hurt because of me."

Paine put his hands on her shoulders. "I have a plan, Abby, but we can't leave them here."

"I know. I'm just afraid for them."

"I promise they'll be okay." Paine ran his finger over her bottom lip. "So stop worrying."

Paine took her hand and headed to the door that George and Agnes went through.

George was in the driver's seat with Agnes in the back. Paine started to protest but then decided it was better to let George drive; this way he had his hands free. He helped Abby in the backseat with Agnes and then ran around and got in the passenger's side. He turned so he could see everyone.

"Okay, this is how we're going to do this." Paine looked at Abby and Agnes. "I want both of you to get down on the floor."

Agnes protested. "I have my gun. You might need my help."

"I appreciate it, Agnes, but I need to know that you and Abby are safe on the floor. That's the best help you could give me." He couldn't do this unless he knew they were safe. He thought she was going to protest, but after a moment she just nodded.

"All right, dear. Don't worry about us." Agnes looked to Abby. "Come on, Abby, let's get hunkered down." Abby frowned. He pleaded with his eyes for her to understand. After a slight hesitation, she ducked down to the floor without saying anything.

Paine turned to George. "Are you sure you want to do this?"

"Well, the way I see it, son, we don't have any other choice," George said, starting the car. "Put your seat belt on, and let's go."

"Right." Paine put his seat belt on and prayed he wasn't making a mistake. "Once you open the garage door, he'll probably come after us fast, so we're going to have to do this quick."

"You concentrate on shooting this guy, and I'll concentrate on driving," George said, looking at Paine. "Together we can get this done."

"Thank you, George." Paine didn't know what else to say.

George put his finger on the garage door opener and then looked at Paine. "Ready?"

Paine checked the backseat one more time to make sure that Abby and Agnes were still on the floor. When he didn't see any heads popping up, he turned back to George. He took a deep breath and nodded.

George nodded back and hit the button on the garage door opener. The door slowly started to rise, and Paine turned to look out the back window. The door was halfway up when he saw a pair of legs come into view.

"Hit it, George!"

"But the door's not up."

"Do it!" Paine yelled.

George hit the gas, and the car jerked backward, hitting the bottom of the door. Paine saw the man jump out of the way.

"Don't stop. Keep going!" Paine couldn't see the man anymore, but he knew they only had a few precious seconds before he was back.

George kept his foot on the gas, still going backward. Paine saw the tree before George did. "Stop!" Paine yelled. George couldn't react fast enough, and they rammed into the tree. Paine felt his teeth rattle.

"Damn, where'd that tree come from?" George said unsteadily.

Paine saw the man getting off the ground, raising his gun to fire.

"Move it, George!"

The first shot rang out, hitting the grille on the front of the car. That was all the encouragement George needed. Putting the car in gear, he turned the wheel and spun out, heading for the road. The second shot hit the back window, shattering it into a million pieces. Paine heard a scream but didn't know if it was Abby or Agnes. The man was running after them, still firing shots. Paine fired a couple shots out the back window. He didn't think he would hit him, but at least it slowed him down. Paine tried to get a good look at the man, but he was wearing some kind of hat. The man kept firing, even though they were out of range. Paine continued to watch him, and he wasn't sure, but it looked like the man was laughing.

"I think we're clear," Paine heard George say.

Paine leaned over the seat. "You ladies all right?"

Agnes was the first one up. "Phew, that was close." Some of her hair had come loose and was hanging in her face. She looked at Paine and then to her husband. "Nice work, dear. I couldn't have done it better myself."

George chuckled, giving her a quick glance. "I'm not so sure about that."

Abby got up from the floor. "You okay?" She asked, reaching over the seat to touch his face.

Paine liked that she was worried about him. He covered her hand with his. "I'm fine, honey." Paine looked into those gorgeous green eyes. She was beautiful. He had a feeling his heart was not going to come out of this clean. It had only been a couple of years since his divorce. Paine had been sure he wouldn't want to be in a relationship for a while after that, but here she was looking at him as if he hung the moon. It scared Paine a little how quickly his feelings for Abby came on, but the thought of not seeing her again scared him more. Whatever it took, he would make sure she was safe, and then they could see what happened next.

"I hate to interrupt, but where are we going?"

George's question brought Paine out of his thoughts. After giving Abby a quick kiss on the mouth, Paine turned back to George. "Do you have family or friends you and Agnes could stay with?"

"I think we need to stay with you until your cop friends get here," George said, glancing at Paine.

"I appreciate the help, George, but I can't ask you to keep putting your life in danger for us."

Abby reached over the seat to touch George's shoulder. "George, I would feel better knowing both of you are safe."

"Abby's right, George," Agnes said, reaching for Abby's hand. "I think Abby's in good hands with Paine."

"I'll take good care of her." Paine smiled at Agnes.

"Well, all right, then. Why don't we go over to Frank and Barbara's?" George looked at Agnes in the rearview mirror.

"That's a good idea. We practice shooting with them once a week."

Paine laughed. "Is there anybody on this island who doesn't know how to shoot?"

"I'm sure there are a few, but I can't name any off the top of my head," George said, deadpan.

Paine chuckled, shaking his head. "Then let's go and meet Frank and Barbara."

Ten minutes later they were pulling into a gravel driveway with pine trees lining the road. George continued down the road, and after a few minutes a two-story brick house came into view. The house wasn't large, but it was surrounded by acres of grass. It was impressive, but Paine was glad he wasn't the one having to mow it.

When they reached the end of the driveway George turned off the car. Paine got out and opened the back door to help Abby and Agnes. He turned toward the house when the front door opened. An older couple came out, smiling. Paine tried not to stare, but the woman couldn't be over four feet tall, and the man had to be at least six feet.

"Agnes, what a surprise," Barbara said.

"Hi, Barbara. I hope you don't mind us just showing up."

"Don't be ridiculous. You know you're always welcome here—" The woman stopped when she saw the car. "What happened to your car?"

"Goodness, George. Do you need to update your eyeglass prescription again?" the older man joked.

"No, Frank. These folks had some trouble," George said, shaking Frank's hand.

Frank turned to look at Paine and Abby. "What kind of trouble?"

"Frank, this is Paine and Abby."

Paine reached out and shook Frank's hand. "I'm sorry, Frank, to barge in on you like this, but George and Agnes need a place to stay for a while."

"Of course they can stay," Frank said, still looking at Paine. "But I'd love to hear what kind of trouble you're in. Am I going to need my gun?"

Paine stood there, speechless, looking at Frank. He turned and looked at Abby and started to laugh. "No, Frank, I don't think you'll need your gun, but I'll let George explain." Paine turned to George. "I'm sorry we can't stay. I think it would be safer for us go."

"Okay, son. You're probably right." George reached into his pocket and took out his cell phone. "Take my phone. Agnes's cell phone number is programmed in there." George handed the phone to Paine. "If you ever need help, just call."

Paine took the phone. "George, I don't know what—"

Before he could finish, Abby was hugging George, crying. "Thank you so much, George."

George hugged her back. "Don't be silly, girl. Anybody else would have done the same thing."

Paine didn't think so but didn't say anything.

Abby let go of George and went to Agnes and hugged her. "Agnes, I don't know how to repay you for everything you've done."

"You're welcome, but as George said, it was nothing," Agnes said through her own tears. "But you have to promise to come visit when this mess is all over."

Paine put his arm around Abby's waist. "Agnes, it will be my pleasure to bring Abby back here." Paine couldn't wait to bring her back when there wasn't a madman chasing them. They could stay at his cabin, and he was sure they could find something to do. Just the thought of what they could do had his pants fitting a little tighter. Paine stepped away from her before he embarrassed himself. "George, I hate to ask, but can we take your car?" Paine looked at the car. The back fender was in the shape of a V from hitting the tree, and the back window was almost completely gone. There were several scrape marks on the trunk and on top of the car. "I'll bring it back good as new."

"Don't you worry about it, son. You just take care of your girl." George tossed the keys to him.

They said their good-byes and got in the car. Paine rolled down the window and leaned out to talk to George. "Remember to stay out of sight. I don't think this guy got a look at you, but just to be on the safe side…"

"We won't leave until we hear from you."

Paine waved and headed down the driveway. At the end of it, he pulled over. "What are you doing?" Abby asked.

"I'm going to call Ben and Jake so they have this number. When they get into town, they can call me." Paine dialed the number and waited for Ben to answer.

"This is Ben."

"Hey, Ben, it's Paine."

"Is there a problem? Whose phone is this?"

"No, we're fine, but I want you to call this number when you get into town."

"Sure thing, Paine. We're getting ready to get on the ferry, so it shouldn't be too much longer."

"Copy that." Paine looked over at Abby. She was looking out the front window, lost in thought. "And Ben?" Paine hesitated for a second. "Thanks." He hung up before Ben could say anything else. Giving Abby a last look, Paine put the car in gear and headed out.

9

Ben looked at the phone in shock.

"What's up?" Jake asked. "And why are you look-ing at the phone as if it grew a head or something?"

"Because Paine just said thanks." Ben shook his head.

"Hmm, that is interesting," Jake said. "I bet it's the girl."

Ben looked at Jake as if he'd lost his mind. "You always assume it's about a girl."

Jake put his hands on his hips. "Then tell me, when was the last time Paine said thanks?"

Ben couldn't think of a time Paine had *ever* said it. "That doesn't mean it has anything to do with the girl."

Jake smiled. "Then put your money where your mouth is. I'll bet you a hundred bucks that his change of attitude has something to do with the girl."

Ben thought about it, then stuck out his hand. "It's a bet."

Jake shook Ben's hand. "I can't wait to meet this girl."

* * *

The Black Angel watched the car speed off. He laughed, shaking his head. This woman had turned out to be very resourceful, and he couldn't help but admire her for it. Whoever this man was helping her; he carried a gun and seemed to handle himself very well. The Black Angel wasn't sure what he would do about the man yet, but the woman was his main concern. He would let the Good Samaritan decide his own fate. He'd lost them for now, but he wasn't concerned. He'd find them again.

The man turned and started walking. The Black Angel was here.

* * *

Abby was startled awake when the car hit a bump.

"Sorry, honey. This road is terrible," Paine said, glancing at her.

Abby sat up straighter in the seat. She looked around to see where they were. The island was really quite beautiful. The pine trees were tall and green, which she assumed was because of all the rain. Once in a while, they would pass an open field. Some had fences around them holding in cows or horses, and in one of them she'd even seen a camel. Now they were driving on a road that ran alongside the ocean. Abby looked out over the water, and she could see other islands.

"Are those islands part of the San Juan Islands?" she asked Paine, still looking at the ocean.

"That's Canada. You can actually take a ferry from Friday Harbor to Victoria."

"I've never been there."

"Well, when this is over, that's just another place we're going to have to visit."

Abby turned to look at Paine. "I know I've said this before, but I'm sorry I got you in this mess."

Paine reached for her hand. "I'm not, Abby." He squeezed her hand. "I know this may sound silly, but I've never been happier."

Abby laughed. "You're happy that we're running from some crazy man who wants to kill us?"

"No, I'm happy that I met you." Paine brought her hand up and kissed the back of it. "I think there's something here between us, and I think you feel it, too."

Abby swallowed, feeling nerves in her stomach. "I do feel it, but is it because you've helped me, and I have this hero-worship thing going on?" Paine started to interrupt her. "Let me finish, Paine." Abby took her hand out of his. "I feel in my heart that's it's real, but until this is over, I think we should just assume it's the hero thing."

Paine reached for her hand again. "Sometimes, Abby, you just have to go with your heart." He kissed her hand again and then let go. "I'll just have to prove to you that it is real."

Abby decided to let the subject drop. "So where are we going?"

Paine gave her a look telling her he knew what she was doing but answered her question anyway. "We're going to the lighthouse, and we'll wait for Jake and Ben to get here."

"Then what?"

"The first thing is we'll go to the sheriff. We'll see what he has to say, and then we'll decide from there."

"But if he can't help us, then what are we going to do?"

"Relax, honey. It's going to be okay," Paine said, glancing at her. "We'll get to the bottom of whatever is going on in this town."

Abby hoped so. She had to be back for school in six days. She could push it to seven, but she had wanted a day to get ready for the next semester. Because she was a kindergarten teacher, some people didn't think there was any planning needed, but Abby always thought it was harder to get ready for kindergarten than other grades. She had to keep the interest of her students, which was hard because their attention span was only good for a couple of minutes. Abby had to come up with some creative ways to teach the alphabet.

"There's the road to the lighthouse," Paine said, bringing Abby back to the present.

They turned onto a paved road and soon were surrounded by trees. They traveled on the road for only a few minutes when they came to a parking lot.

"We walk from here." Paine got out of the car. Before Abby could get her car door open, Paine was there. He opened it and helped her out.

"Thanks." Abby looked around and didn't see many cars in the parking lot. "It doesn't seem to be too crowded."

"It's the off-season right now. We have some time before Ben and Jake get here. Do you want to go see it?" Paine asked her.

"Do you think it's safe?"

"It's okay, Abby. He doesn't know where we are, and there are still some tourists here." Paine took her hand and started down the dirt path.

"So what do you know about this lighthouse?" asked Abby.

"I know it got its name from the lime kilns that were built in the area in the eighteen sixties." Paine looked down at her. "And in whale season, it's the best place to see the whales."

Abby got excited at that. "When is whale season?"

Paine laughed at her enthusiasm. "It's usually between May and October. We're probably too late, but occasionally there's one or two left. So if we're lucky, we might be able to catch sight of some."

"Well, let's go then," Abby said, pulling on Paine.

After a few minutes on the path, Abby caught her first sight of the lighthouse. The tower of the lighthouse was attached to a small white house. Abby assumed at some point the house was used for the lighthouse keeper.

"It's built on solid rock and stands twenty feet above the water," Paine said.

"We probably can't go to the top," Abby said.

Paine chuckled. "No, it's closed to the public now."

As they got closer, Abby had to tilt her head to look at the tower. She would see a light blink every few seconds. They'd spent twenty minutes looking and talking about the lighthouse when Abby noticed a few people looking out at the water and pointing.

"Let's go see what they're looking at." Paine reached again for Abby's hand.

Even before they reached the edge of the rock, Abby saw the whales. Two humpback whales were about a hundred feet away. It always awed Abby that something that big could move with so much grace. "They're beautiful," she whispered.

Paine put his arm around her shoulders, and they stood there watching the whales in silence. Abby didn't know how long they stood there before she felt the chill of the wind. Agnes had lent her a coat, but Abby couldn't help from shivering.

"Come on. Let's go back to the car so we can get you warmed up." Abby didn't argue. She was freezing. The wind had picked up, and it looked to Abby like it was going to rain again. They had just reached the car when the first raindrops fell. Paine turned on the car and cranked the heat.

"It shouldn't take too long for it to heat up."

"Last night in the rain, I thought I wouldn't ever be that cold again." Abby rubbed her hands together to get them warm. "So today isn't so bad."

"Can you tell me anything else about last night?" Paine asked. "Do you remember anything new?"

Abby thought about it. "I don't think so, Paine. My car died. I got out and started walking. Then I came upon those two men." Abby shuddered at the thought of last night.

Paine took her hands into his and started rubbing them. "It's okay, Abby. We'll get this figured out, and then you can go back to Portland and get on with your life."

Abby looked up at Paine. "Do you think it will be that simple?" she asked hopefully.

"Until we know for sure what's going on, I really don't know."

Abby hoped and prayed it would be simple. She was so tired and scared. She wanted things to be normal again.

"So what's your life like back in Portland? What do you do besides teach kindergarten?" Paine asked. "How about your family?"

"My parents live in Spokane, Washington." Abby smiled, thinking about her parents. "They are both retired, but you wouldn't know it. My dad can't sit still for more than a minute, and my mom is always telling him to relax."

"Did you grow up in Spokane?"

"No, we lived in Portland while I was growing up. My parents just recently moved to Spokane." Abby chuckled. "They said they were tired of all the rain in Portland. Now they have to deal with the snow. I'm not sure why they didn't move to somewhere warmer."

"You sound like you're close to them. Any brothers or sisters?"

"No, it's just me. My parents had me later in life. I think if they could have, they would have had more, but my dad said that after having me, they didn't think they would be lucky in getting two perfect children." Abby leaned her head back to rest on the seat. "I should probably call them, but I don't want to worry them."

"When we get to the sheriff's office, you could probably give them a call."

"I will." Abby yawned.

"Come over here," Paine said.

Abby turned her head, giving him a questioning look. "Why?"

Paine smiled. "Relax, honey. You can rest your head against my shoulder." When Abby didn't move, Paine reached for her. "You're obviously tired, Abby. I promise I'll behave."

"What about you?" Abby asked, moving to get closer to him.

"I'm fine. I'm used to operating on not much sleep." Paine lifted his arm so Abby could get closer. Once Abby was settled, Paine rested his arm on her shoulders. "Get some rest. Ben and Jake should be here soon."

"I don't think I'll be able to sleep."

"That's okay. Just rest."

Abby's last thought before falling asleep was how nice and safe she felt at that moment.

10

Paine sat there holding Abby, thinking about her. He wanted her, and if he admitted it to himself, it made him nervous and excited at the same time. His ex-wife had burned him. He had thought that when he married, he would be married for life. His ex didn't see it that way, though. They had lasted for five years when things went south. She had told Paine that he was never around, and she needed more. Paine knew his job took a lot of his time, but his job was what made him who he was. If he wasn't a cop, he had no idea what he would do.

Abby shifted, snuggling closer to Paine. Her left breast was touching his chest. Paine got hard. He knew he had it bad if a single touch turned him on.

Trying to think of other things, Paine checked his watch. Ben and Jake should be here anytime now. It was getting dark, and he really didn't want to spend another night out in the open. Paine thought about last night. *How did he find us so quickly?* He found them first at the cabin and then again at George and Agnes's. Even if he was good tracker, it had rained most of the night. Their footprints should have been washed away. So how did he do it?

Paine was still trying to figure it out when he saw a set of headlights pulling into the parking lot. He tensed for a moment but relaxed when he saw Jake's blond head in the passenger side of the car.

Paine sat up. Abby sat up in alarm. "It's okay, Abby. It's Ben and Jake." Paine opened the car door. "Wait here, honey. Stay warm, and I'll be right back."

He saw Ben and Jake getting out of their car. Paine walked over and shook hands with each man. "Can't tell you how happy I am to see you two."

"Well, it's nice to be wanted," Jake joked.

"What the hell are you mixed up in?" Ben asked.

"I'm not sure yet, Ben." Paine looked over at Abby. "Abby showed up at my door last night. Somebody was chasing her, and the next thing I know, we're being shot at. So I got us the hell out of there, and we've been running ever since."

Jake poked his elbow into Ben's arm. "I told you it was a girl."

Paine frowned at Jake but didn't say anything.

"What's the plan then?" Ben asked.

"I want to go to the sheriff and tell him what's happened." He ran his fingers through his hair. "I'm not sure how much help he'll be, but whatever happens, Abby is never to be left alone. That's why I wanted you here. I don't trust anyone in this town."

"So we go to the sheriff. Then what? He's not going to want cops from Portland poking around in his town," Jake said.

"I don't care if he likes it or not. I'm not leaving Abby with him and then saying good luck," Paine said tersely.

"Hey, I'm on your side, Paine," Jake said.

"I know, Jake. Sorry about that."

Ben and Jake looked at each other.

"Let's get in the car, and you can meet Abby."

The men walked over to the car. Paine got in the driver's seat, and the other two climbed into the back.

Paine made the introductions. "Abby, this is Ben and Jake."

Abby shook each man's hand. "It's nice to meet you both."

"So we hear you've had some trouble." Ben smiled.

Abby laughed. "You could say that." She looked at Paine. "Unfortunately for Paine, I showed up on his doorstep."

Paine reached over and squeezed her hand. It didn't go unnoticed by Ben and Jake.

"Now, it looks like you both also get to be a part of it," Abby said, grimacing.

"Think nothing of it, darlin'—we like trouble." Jake winked at her.

Paine felt a moment of jealousy. He knew Jake was a relentless flirt and didn't mean anything by it, but it didn't stop Paine from wanting to punch him in the face.

"Abby why don't you tell Ben and Jake about last night." Abby nodded and told her story again. Paine listened to see if there was anything different she might tell without realizing it.

"The man who shot the other man had some kind of accent."

"What kind of accent?" Ben asked.

"I'm not sure, but if I had to guess, I would say Russian or something close to that."

Ben looked at Paine. "Any ideas?"

Paine shrugged. "I have no idea. It could be a drug deal gone wrong, or maybe they just didn't like each other. We'll figure it out though."

Abby nodded and smiled at Paine.

I sure hope we can figure it out, because I know this guy is not going to stop until he has Abby, Paine thought.

He turned back to Ben and Jake. "Follow us back to town. We'll meet with the sheriff and decide what to do after that."

Ben and Jake nodded and got out of the car.

Paine reached to put the car in gear when he felt Abby's hand on his arm. He looked at her.

"I don't know how I'm ever going to repay you." Abby said quietly. "You've risked your life for me, and I can't thank you enough for that."

Paine's heart flipped again. He gently drew her closer and lowered his head to kiss her. It was just a whisper of a kiss. He drew back. "You don't have to thank me, Abby. You can, however, repay me by going out to dinner with me when this is all over."

Abby smiled. "Deal."

They were sitting there looking at each other when they heard a horn go off. Paine turned and looked over at the other car. Ben and Jake were grinning at him.

Paine gave them a dirty look, but he let go of Abby and put the car in gear.

"I like them," Abby said.

Paine glanced at her. "They're good cops. I trust them with my life."

"How long have you worked with them?"

"When I became a captain, I ended up in their precinct. That was six years ago." Paine looked in his rearview mirror and saw Ben and Jake keeping close.

"You're a captain?"

Paine smiled. "Yep."

"I'm impressed. It also explains some things."

Paine frowned at her. "What do you mean?"

"It explains why you're so bossy," Abby said teasingly.

Paine smiled. "Yes, I suppose I am bossy." Then he laughed.

"What?" Abby asked.

"It's funny because I thought the same thing about you."

Abby grinned. "Okay, so we're both boss—"

Before Abby could finish her sentence, the side window shattered. She screamed.

"Abby, get down!" Paine yelled. Paine swore, turning the steering wheel right and driving the car in a ditch. The back window shattered next. "Damn it." Paine threw himself across the seat to cover Abby. He pushed her down to the floor. "Are you all right?" Abby didn't say anything. Paine lifted his head to look at her. She was pale and looked scared. "Abby," he said louder. "Are you hurt?"

Abby shook her head. "How did he find us?" she asked frightened.

That's a very good question, Paine thought.

"Paine?" He heard Ben yelling.

"We're fine," Paine yelled back. "Can you see anything?"

"No, but I'm guessing he's shooting from those trees over there."

Paine lifted his head to peer out the window. There was an open field and then a line of trees. They were at least five hundred yards away. Whoever this was would have to have a high-powered rifle and be a very good shot to hit a moving car. Drug dealers weren't usually that skilled. *I could be wrong, but something feels off.*

Paine looked at Abby. "We're going to have move, Abby. We can't stay here like sitting ducks."

"I know," she whispered.

Paine opened the passenger door and got out, keeping his head down. He saw Ben and Jake about ten feet away, squatting down behind their own car. "We're going to come to you. When I say, start shooting at the trees."

"Copy that, Paine," Ben said.

He turned back to Abby. "Okay, honey. We're going to go to the other car."

She looked up at him with frightened eyes but nodded. Paine was sure his heart just flipped all the way over this time.

He reached for her hand to help her out. "Keep your head down and do exactly as I tell you."

Paine knew he sounded like a jackass, but he was scared, and he couldn't let anything happen to her. Once Abby was out of the car, they inched closer to the bumper of the car. A shot rang out above their heads.

"This guy is persistent. I'll give him that," Jake said.

Paine squeezed Abby's hand, and she turned to look at him. "When Ben and Jake start shooting, we're going to make a run for their car. It's not that far."

Abby nodded.

"You stay on my left side and don't stop." Paine bent his head and gave her a quick kiss. "No matter what, you keep your ass moving."

"I got it, bossy," Abby said, annoyed.

Paine smiled and then looked to Ben and Jake. "Okay, we're ready."

Ben and Jake nodded and started shooting. Abby covered her ears from the noise, and he put his arm around her waist, trying to keep his body in front of hers. Bent over, they started for the other car. They were almost there when Paine felt a sharp pain in his arm. Not slowing down, he kept pushing Abby toward the car. He let out a breath when they reached it. He quickly opened the back passenger door and put Abby inside with Paine right behind her. "Keep down, Abby, and don't move."

"Paine, you're bleeding," Abby said in alarm. "Why are you bleeding?"

"It's okay, honey. He just nicked me. I'm fine."

"But you're bleeding." She looked a little queasy.

"Ben, Jake, get in here!" Paine yelled.

The shooting stopped, and Ben and Jake got in the front seat, keeping their heads down. Paine couldn't see them but knew they were in the car.

"Now what, Paine?" Jake asked excitedly.

"Ben, do you think you could drive if Jake and I did the shooting?"

"Copy that, Paine."

Another shot rang out, hitting the side window again and sending shattered glass flying everywhere.

"Damn, this guy is starting to annoy me." This came from Jake.

"We're only going to have one shot at this," Paine said anxiously. "Jake, can you get back here?"

"No problem."

Paine could hear the front door opening and then closing, and seconds later the back door was opening. Jake jumped in as another shot rang out. He quickly scooted over the seat to the other side, still keeping his head down.

"Okay, Abby, slide under me so we can trade places." Even in the dangerous situation they were in, his body still reacted having Abby under him. Luckily for him, she moved quickly and was soon situated on the other side. "When we start shooting, Ben, get us the hell out of here."

"You don't have to tell me twice."

Paine looked at Abby. "Keep your head down, honey." Not waiting for her to answer, Paine looked at Jake. "You ready?"

Jake nodded. "Ready."

When they started shooting, Ben put the car in gear and hit the gas. Paine swore when more shots hit the car. *Damn! Who is this guy?* They kept shooting until they had gone down the road for several minutes.

"I think we're clear," Ben said.

Paine sat back in the seat and reached for Abby down on the floor. "Are you okay?" Paine asked, his heart pounding.

"I'm fine, Paine," Abby said shakily, sitting next to him and reaching for his arm. "You're the one who's hurt."

"I told you, Abby, it's fine." Paine tried to pull his arm back.

"Stop moving. Let me look at it," Abby said firmly.

"It's okay, Abby. I know how you feel about blood."

"Stop moving," she said, annoyed.

Paine sighed and stopped moving. He looked over at Jake and saw him grinning. "What?" he asked irritably.

"Nothing." Jake smirked.

"Jake, give me your shirt," Abby said in the same tone as before.

Paine grinned when he saw Jake frown. "You heard her. Give her your shirt." After a slight hesitation, Jake laughed and handed it to her, leaving him in only his T-shirt.

Abby took the shirt and started wrapping Paine's arm. "I don't think you'll need stitches, but it really needs to be cleaned out." When she was done, she looked at Paine. "That's all I can do for now. But when we get to civilization, you need to see a doctor."

"Thanks, Abby." Paine lifted her hand and kissed the back of it. He felt Abby trying to pull her hand out of his, but he didn't let go. He needed to touch her, just to make sure she was safe.

"Are we still heading to the sheriff's office?" Ben asked from the front.

Paine thought about it. Somehow the shooter had found them. Paine still didn't understand that. *How did he find them?* A thought occurred to Paine. He looked at Abby. "Did you have any contact with this guy at all last night? Did he ever get near you? I mean close enough to touch you?"

"No, Paine." She did take her hand away then, and Paine didn't stop her. He missed her warmth. "I told you everything that happened." Abby frowned. "Why are you asking me this?"

Then how is this guy tracking them? Paine had made sure nobody had followed them to the lighthouse. When they had pulled out of the lighthouse, he didn't see any cars. Somehow, though, this guy knew where they were.

"Paine?"

The only thing that makes sense is some kind of tracking device, but she said the guy didn't get near her. "Where's your phone?" he asked abruptly.

"I lost it last night in the rain. Why?"

Okay, so it wasn't her phone. Paine knew she was being tracked, but how?

"Paine, answer me, damn it." Abby was clearly irritated now.

Paine looked at her. "I'm sorry, honey." He reached for her hand again. "This guy always seems to be just one step behind us. He has to be tracking you somehow."

Abby frowned. "You mean like some kind of bug."

"How could he have done that, Paine, if he didn't get anywhere near her?" Ben asked, looking in his rear-view mirror at him.

Paine ran his hand through his hair. "Hell, I don't know."

"I say we go to the sheriff's office as we planned. At least we'll be around people and not sitting out here in the open," Jake said.

Paine nodded. "Okay, we go to the sheriff, tell him what happened, and then find somewhere safe to keep Abby."

The man watched the car speed away. He shook his head. This woman was starting to become his obsession. The Black Angel had to remind himself that she was just a job, but he couldn't stop feeling a little sad that in the end, she would be dead. He knew he could have killed her then, but he had wanted to have a little more fun. He wanted her scared. Even though there were three men trying to protect the woman now, it didn't worry him. They just made it more of a challenge. He watched as the taillights faded into the night. "My sweet Abby. The Black Angel is here."

11

Abby was exhausted. She wasn't sure how much more her nerves could take. After the shootout in the car, she couldn't stop shaking. She tried to hide it from Paine but didn't think she was doing a very good job. He kept looking at her and asking her if she was okay. Abby swore if he asked her one more time, she was going to punch him in the nose. She knew he was just concerned, but she didn't think she could hide it for much longer. She needed to be alone for just a little while. She needed some time to decompress and maybe even cry.

"We're coming into town," Ben said.

She looked around. Even though it wasn't that late, the whole town looked like it had already gone to bed.

"Everything looks closed," Abby said.

"It's okay, honey. The sheriff will probably still be there," Paine said. "Even in a small town, there's always paperwork to be done."

How much paperwork could there be? Abby thought. *The town's dead.* Abby cringed. *Bad choice of words, Abby.*

"There's the sheriff's office." Paine pointed to an old brick building. Ben parked in an empty spot in front. Abby reached for the door handle, but Paine stopped her. "Let Ben and Jake go first." Too tired to argue, Abby nodded. She watched as Ben and Jake got out and walked around the car to her door. They stood on each side of it. "Okay, Abby. I want you to slowly get out of the car, and I'll be right behind you."

"Do you think he's here already?" Abby asked, trying to fight off the panic she felt.

"No, honey. I think it's safe. I just want to be careful." Paine slid his finger down her cheek. "I'm not going to let anything happen to you. I promise."

Abby nodded and turned to the door before she made a total fool out of herself by crying. Opening the car door, she stepped out with Paine right behind her and Ben and Jake at her sides. She noticed Ben and Jake were looking in all directions. Together they walked up the stairs to the glass door.

Once they were inside, Abby looked around. There were four desks sitting in the middle of the room. They were positioned so two of the desks faced the other two. There was a hallway to the left, but Abby couldn't see where it went.

At first Abby didn't see anyone. Then they all turned to the hallway when they heard a door closing. Abby could hear footsteps coming toward them. She could feel Paine tense up behind her. Ben and Jake moved so that they stood in front of her.

"Oh," she heard someone say. Abby couldn't see who it was, because Ben and Jake were too tall to see over. "I didn't know anybody had come in." The voice sounded young and friendly.

Paine stepped around them. "Are you the sheriff?" Paine asked.

"I am," the voice said. "I'm Sheriff Yates, but you can call me David. What can I do for you?"

Ben and Jake moved, and Abby got her first look at the sheriff. He was young. Abby would put him in his late twenties. He had light-brown hair, and Abby was pretty sure that the highlights in it were not natural. He was medium build and had a handsome face.

"I'm Mark Paine, and this is Ben, Jake, and Abby," Paine said, looking back at them.

The sheriff looked at Ben and Jake and then stopped at Abby. "Hello, miss."

Abby noticed the interest in his eyes.

Paine put his arm around her. "We've had some trouble and need your help."

The sheriff looked at her and then at Paine. Giving her a small smile, he looked back at Paine. "What kind of trouble?"

"There's a man out there trying to kill Abby."

The sheriff looked at Abby again. "Oh, and why's that?"

"Do you think we can sit somewhere, and we'll tell you the whole story?" Paine asked.

"Sure. Come on back to my office."

Paine turned to Ben and Jake. "You guys wait here and keep an eye out."

They both nodded and went to the window. They looked out at the streets.

Paine put his hand on Abby's elbow, and they followed the sheriff down the hallway. Abby noticed a couple of rooms off the hallway, but the doors were closed. They were almost to the end of the hall before the sheriff stopped in front of an open door. He stepped aside so that Abby and Paine could go in first.

It wasn't a large office. There was enough room for a filing cabinet, a desk, and two chairs sitting in front of it.

"Have a seat." The sheriff gestured to the two chairs. "So why don't you tell me what's going on?"

"First, I should tell you that I'm a captain for the Portland Police Department," Paine said, reaching for his badge and handing it to the sheriff. "Ben and Jake are detectives in my precinct."

The sheriff took the badge but barely glanced at it before handing it back to Paine. "I don't understand. Why are they here?" The sheriff frowned. "Are they here on a case? And if so, why wasn't I notified?"

"I called them."

"You called them rather than coming to me? The sheriff?" Abby could see the sheriff was starting to get angry.

"It's nothing personal, Sheriff. I don't know you."

The sheriff looked at Paine and then Abby, and then back to Paine. "Why don't you tell me what's going on?"

"I was here vacationing when last night Abby knocked on my door." Paine reached for her hand and entwined his fingers with hers.

The sheriff looked at their entwined hands. "And Abby is your wife? Girlfriend?" The sheriff asked.

"We didn't even know each other before last night."

The sheriff was back to frowning. Abby understood his confusion. She and Paine seemed closer than two people should be, considering they'd just met last night.

"Abby saw a man shoot another man."

The sheriff looked at her. "Do you know these men?"

"No."

"Then how did you happen to see a man shoot another man?"

Sighing, Abby started her story. The sheriff interrupted once in a while to ask a question or two. By the time she was done, Abby felt mentally drained.

At first the sheriff didn't say anything. He was leaning back in his chair with his arms crossed. Abby was starting to feel a little self-conscious under his scrutiny. After a few seconds of silence, the sheriff sat forward again.

"Can you describe these men? You saw their faces?"

"Yes. I didn't see the man who got shot that well, but I could give you a pretty good description of the man who shot him."

"And where did this shooting take place?"

Abby looked at Paine.

"Sheriff, Abby's not from around here. It was dark, and as she told you, she was lost to begin with."

"I understand, *Captain*, but I have a dead body somewhere," The sheriff said, looking at Abby. "You can't give me any clues as to where I should start looking?"

The sheriff's tone made Abby's temper rise. "Look, Sheriff. I was a little busy running for my life. I'm sorry

I didn't leave bread crumbs for you to follow back to the body."

Sighing, the sheriff said, "I'm sorry, Abby. I didn't mean to be such an ass, but we don't have murders here."

"We haven't told you the rest of the story yet, Sheriff," Paine said.

The sheriff looked at Paine. "There's more than a murder?" His voice rose.

Paine filled him in on the shooter finding them in the cabin and then again at George and Agnes's house. He also described the earlier shooting in the car. "I made sure we weren't followed. Somehow this guy can always find us."

"He probably just tracked you to the cabin and then to George's place."

"I would agree if he hadn't found us at the lighthouse. He was waiting for us when we left the lighthouse parking lot."

"Well, then, what are you saying?"

"I'm not sure," Paine admitted. "I haven't gotten it all figured out yet."

"We'll get to the bottom of it." The sheriff stood. "First thing in the morning, we'll go over some details on where to look. We can probably get close, based on where your cabin is and how far Abby ran before she got to you. Meanwhile, I'll take Abby into protective custody."

Paine stood up then. "No!"

"What do you mean, no?" The sheriff was clearly angry now. "She is a witness to a crime in *my* jurisdiction, and I'm taking her into protective custody."

"Sorry, Sheriff, that's not going to happen," Paine said in a deadly voice.

"You have no jurisdiction here. I appreciate you bringing her here, but now you can get back to your vacation."

Abby stood, too tense to sit anymore. "Sheriff, I'd rather stay with Paine."

The sheriff turned his angry eyes to her. "Sorry, Abby. You don't have a choice."

Abby was starting to protest when they heard a commotion from the front. The sheriff came around his desk, heading for the door.

"Wait here, Abby."

And then Paine was gone, shutting the door behind him. Abby could hear yelling. The first voice she didn't recognize, but the second voice was Ben's. Abby went to the door and opened it a crack so she could hear more clearly.

"Let me go right this minute," The unfamiliar voice was saying.

"What are you doing?" Abby heard the sheriff say.

"This gentleman came in and started heading down the hall. We asked him very politely to stop, but he didn't," Jake said.

"Do you know who I am?" The man was still yelling.

"Nope," Jake said.

"I'm John Yates, you jackass."

"Still don't know who you are," Jake said.

"That's my father," the sheriff said. "You can let him go."

"Who are these men, David? Can't you keep control of your own department?" the father said unkindly.

"Dad, these men are detectives from Portland." Abby thought the sheriff sounded apologetic. She wasn't sure what he would be sorry for.

"I don't care who they are. These goons here attacked me, and I'm going to press charges."

Jake snorted. "Go ahead, mister."

"Dad, these people had some trouble, and they were just trying to protect Abby."

He was still yelling. "Who in the hell is Abby?"

Abby was tired of sitting on the sidelines. Stepping out, she quickly walked down the hallway and stopped next to Paine. "That would be me." All the men turned to look at her. "Abby Turner. It's nice to meet you, Mr. Yates," she said, holding out her hand and waiting for the man to shake it.

He only hesitated for a second before lifting his hand and shaking hers. "You'll have to excuse me. I'm not used to being treated that way."

"There's nothing to excuse, Mr. Yates, but these men are just trying to protect me," Abby said sweetly. The man's behavior was inexcusable, but Abby didn't want him getting Ben and Jake in trouble. Abby figured his suit cost him more than she made in a month. He was just as tall as his son, and she guessed he used to be as handsome, but his nastiness had washed those looks away long ago. All Abby could see now was a rich, egotistical man who was used to getting his way.

He straightened his tie. "And what exactly do you need protecting from, young lady?"

The sheriff stepped in front of his father. "Dad, it's police business."

The older Yates glared at his son. "Don't forget who you're talking to, boy." He took a step closer to his son. "And don't forget how you got to be sheriff."

The sheriff's face turned red with anger. Abby almost felt sorry for him.

"I haven't forgotten, Dad, but it's still police business," the sheriff said through clenched teeth.

Abby watched both men, holding her breath, waiting to see who was going to throw the first punch. She didn't think there was any love lost between the two men.

Paine stepped between father and son and looked at the younger Yates. "Sheriff, you can work out your family issues later. Right now, though, we have bigger problems."

The sheriff gave his father one last look and nodded. "You're right." He stepped back and looked at Abby. "As I said before, I'll put Abby in protective custody."

"Sorry, Sheriff, I'm not going to let you do that," Paine said menacingly.

"Are you going to let him talk to you that way?" the older Yates said nastily. "What kind of sheriff are you, anyway?"

At first the sheriff didn't say anything. He looked at his father and then turned to Paine. "Okay, detective, you win."

The older Yates started sputtering. "Be a man, boy! Take control—"

"Shut up, Dad!" he said while looking at Paine. "There's a motel up the road. It's not fancy, but you'll be comfortable there for the night." He then turned to Abby. "Tomorrow morning we'll head out to look for the body."

"Body! What body?" the older man yelled.

"We'll be here at eight." Paine said taking Abby's elbow. They followed Ben and Jake out the door. Abby could hear Mr. Yates yelling at his son.

When they were in the car with Abby and Paine in the backseat, Jake turned to look back at them. "Remind me to call my father later and say thank you. What an asshole."

"Ben, tomorrow I want you to find out everything you can about Mr. Yates. How he got his money, who he associates with," Paine said.

Ben nodded. "You think he has something to do with this?"

"I have no idea. Just trying to cover all the bases." He looked at Abby. "And for that matter, find out what you can about the sheriff."

"You don't think the sheriff is in on it, do you?" Abby was surprised.

"I don't know, honey, but something is off with those two."

"Just because they don't get along doesn't make them guilty of anything," Abby said. "You'd have to investigate half the country otherwise."

"I know, but they're all I've got for now." Paine looked to Ben. "Let's get to the motel and get some rest."

Abby rested her head against the backseat. As tired as she was, she didn't think she would be able to sleep. Her mind was going in all sorts of directions. *Who is this guy? How does he keep finding us? And most of all, when will this be over?*

It didn't take them long to reach the motel. It had two levels, with rooms running down the length of the building on each level. It was old but looked like it was well maintained.

"Okay, we're all going to go in," Paine said. "Abby, just like before, you wait for Ben and Jake, and I'll be behind you."

They reached the lobby without incident. It looked like the rest of the building—old but clean. Paine stepped up to the counter and rang the bell. A couple of seconds later, an older woman emerged. She was tall and thin with white hair. Abby had to hide her smile. She was wearing the brightest pink jogging outfit Abby had ever seen. The woman came up to the counter.

"Hello there." Her voice was raspy like she had a sore throat. "What can I do for you?"

"We need a couple of rooms," Paine said.

"Not a problem. Are you here on vacation?"

"Something like that. Do you have two adjoining rooms with two beds in each?"

Abby frowned. *Just two rooms?* She started to say something, but Paine shook his head at her.

"Sure. It's seventy-five for each room." Paine paid with cash and took the keys from her. "They're on the second floor. Rooms twenty-one and twenty-two."

Paine thanked her, and they headed for the door. Once again she was surrounded. They took the stairs that led up to the second floor and stopped in front of the first two doors. Paine handed a key to Jake. "You guys take the first room. Abby and I will take the second."

Abby tried to protest, but Paine was already leading her to the second room. "Remember that conservation we had about being bossy?" Abby said, irritated. She heard Jake chuckle.

"Yes, we agreed we were both bossy. Remember?"

Paine unlocked the door. He stepped in, flicked on the light, and moved aside so Abby could enter the room. The first thing Abby noticed was the carpet. It was green shag that looked as if it had just stepped out of the eighties. The two beds were covered with floral-print bedspreads. *At least it's not orange roses,* Abby thought, thinking back to the last room they'd shared.

Paine shut the door and went to the other door that opened to the adjoining room. Jake was waiting on the other side, smiling. "Does anyone else feel like there should be a disco ball on the ceiling?"

Ben came over to stand next to Jake. "I'm going to move the car around to the back."

Paine nodded. "Good idea. Jake, go with him and check out the area. Then come back here, and we'll make a game plan."

They both nodded and headed out.

"You know, you could have at least asked me if I wanted my own room," Abby said, annoyed.

"There's no way in hell, Abby, that I'm leaving you alone."

"I don't have a say?" Abby tried to hold back tears. She needed to be alone, just for a little while.

"No."

"Fine!" Abby turned and walked to the bathroom and slammed the door. She knew she was acting like a child, but she couldn't help it. She yanked off her coat and threw it to the floor. Then she burst into tears. She grabbed a washcloth to cover her mouth so Paine wouldn't hear her.

12

Paine watched Abby storm off. He couldn't blame her for being mad, but he wasn't going to leave her alone. She would just have to get over it.

Paine went to the window and looked out to make sure everything was clear, and that's when he heard her. Abby was crying. It was muffled, but he knew she was crying. His heart twisted in his chest. His first reaction was to go to her, but he stopped himself. *Would she want me to? Or should I just let her cry it out?* He felt like a fish out of water. His ex-wife cried because she wanted the attention, but he didn't think Abby would do that.

Paine was still deciding what to do when he heard the water turn on. He went back to the window and let her be. A few minutes later, Ben and Jake walked into their own room. Paine met them at the adjoining door. "Did you see anything?"

Ben spoke first. "It seems to be quiet. I parked the car close to the building in the back, in case we need to get to it."

"I walked the perimeter but didn't see anything," Jake said. "There are no new cars in the parking lot."

Paine turned and walked over to the only table in the room. Ben and Jake followed him. There were only two chairs, so Paine and Jake sat down while Ben stood.

"So what's the game plan for tomorrow?" Jake asked.

As Paine started to answer, the bathroom door opened, and Abby walked out. She stopped midstep when she saw them sitting there. "Oh, sorry. I didn't mean to interrupt."

Her nose and eyes were red from crying, but Paine still thought she was beautiful. He stood and walked over to her. When he was in front of her, he reached up and brushed the corner of her eye with his finger. "It's okay." He said it quietly so that only she could hear. She blinked at him, looking lost. Paine didn't care who was in the room. He bent and kissed her softly on the lips. "It's okay," he whispered again. Then he took her hand and led her over to the chair where he'd been sitting.

Once she was seated, he looked at Ben and Jake. They were smiling at him. He shrugged and smiled back. He laughed when he saw the stunned expressions on their faces.

Abby looked up at him. "What's so funny?"

"Nothing, honey. We were just discussing what the plan is tomorrow."

"So what is the plan?" she asked.

Paine sat down on the closest bed. "We go with the sheriff tomorrow and try to find the body. We need to know who he is first so we know where to start to figure this thing out." He ran a hand through his hair. "Ben will start working on getting background on the sheriff and his father. Jake will go with us." Too antsy to sit, Paine stood. "And then we'll see where we go after that." He looked at Abby. She was staring out into space, chewing on her lower lip. He went over to her and knelt in front of her. "Abby, we'll figure this out. I promise."

"I know, Paine." Abby touched his arm. Then she jumped up, almost knocking him over. "Damn it, Paine. I forgot about your arm."

Paine stood. "It's fine, Abby."

Ignoring him, Abby looked over at Ben and Jake. "I need ointment and bandages."

Jake stood. "I saw a Walgreens just around the corner."

"I'll go with Jake and get us some food," Ben said.

"Good, and get some aspirin, too," Abby said, walking into the bathroom.

Jake and Ben looked at Paine.

"What?" Paine asked.

"Nothing, boss. I like her," Ben said.

"Me, too. It's fun to see you getting bossed around," Jake said grinning.

Paine scowled at him. "I am not getting bossed around."

Abby walked out of the bathroom. "Paine, sit on the bed."

Jake snorted.

"Why haven't you guys left yet?" Abby looked at Jake and Ben.

"Yeah, why haven't you guys left yet?" Paine repeated, grinning.

Ben laughed. "We're out of here."

"Be careful," Paine said seriously.

Both men nodded and left. Paine turned to Abby. She was standing over by one of the beds, holding a wet cloth in her hand and waiting for him.

Paine walked over and sat down. Abby knelt down in front of him and started unwrapping Jake's shirt from his arm. "You really should see a doctor."

"I told you, Abby, it's just a scratch."

Paine sucked in air when Abby removed the shirt.

Abby gagged. "Oh man, I hope I don't puke."

Paine looked down at his arm. There was a cut about two inches long. It was bleeding, but not too badly. He looked at Abby. She had gone pale and did look like she was going to throw up. "Abby, let me do it," Paine said, reaching for the wet cloth.

"No, I'm fine. I'll do it."

Paine watched her as she started wiping the blood away from the cut. She was biting on her lip again. Her hair was hanging in front of her face, so he reached over and put a curl behind her ear. She looked up at him. Neither said anything. Paine slowly lowered his head and covered her mouth with his. He could taste the salt from her tears on her lips, and it reminded him she had been crying earlier. He moved his mouth down her jawline, kissing every inch.

"We're alone now, Abby." He wanted her. Now. He started to reach for the button of her shirt, but Abby reached up and stopped him. Paine leaned back so he could see her. "What's wrong?" He was breathing hard, and his pants were too damn tight.

"I think we should stop," Abby said, breathing just as hard. "It won't take that long for Jake and Ben to get food."

Paine rested his forehead against hers. "You're right. I want you, Abby."

"I want you, too."

Paine kissed her again. He brought his legs around her waist to draw her closer.

Abby reached up and put her arms around him. "We have to stop," Abby whispered.

"I know. Just a little longer." Paine reached under her shirt to feel her bare skin, and he swore his own skin had just caught fire. He inched his hand up higher and covered her breast. "You're perfect, Abby." With his other hand he started unbuttoning her pants. He felt Abby covering his hand to stop.

"Paine, we can't do this now."

Paine knew she was right, but it didn't stop him from getting one more kiss. He brought his mouth down hard onto hers. He sneaked his tongue in and tasted her. She opened for him willingly. Paine was so turned on now, he didn't know if he would be able to stop. He heard a moan come from her. He pulled back, breathing hard. "You're right, Abby. We better stop while we still can."

Abby looked up at him with both longing and regret. "Can you believe I was the one stopping us this time?"

Paine chuckled. "Believe me, Abby, I didn't want to stop the other times either." He reached up and gently touched her cheek. "I promise, though, the next time I won't stop."

Paine heard the door opening in the next room. "I think they're back."

Abby jumped up and went back into the bathroom. Paine hid his smile.

In the bathroom, Abby ran some water over her face. She was sure it was flushed from the make-out session. She'd had never been kissed like that, and she hadn't wanted it to stop. The man knew what he was doing in the kissing department. Abby couldn't wait for what came next.

Paine also knew she had been crying. She appreciated the fact that he'd left her alone. Abby wasn't sure she could have kept it together if he had come in.

She heard the men talking in the next room. Abby knew she couldn't stay in the bathroom forever. She looked at herself in the mirror one last time. She had dark circles under her eyes, which were still a little red from crying. Nothing she could do about it now. Shrugging, she opened the door.

Abby stepped in the room. Paine was sitting at the table with Ben, and Jake was on the bed.

"The guys brought hamburgers." Paine reached in a white bag to get one out. Abby inhaled. It smelled wonderful. She had forgotten how hungry she was. She moved to the table to get it from Paine when Ben stood.

"Here, Abby, you sit," Ben said, moving over to the second bed.

"Thanks, Ben." Abby sat and took the burger from Paine. He winked. Abby felt that awful flush start again. *Get a grip, Abby.* She took a big bite of her hamburger. *Heavenly.*

"Have you talked to Kate lately?" Jake asked.

Kate? Who is Kate? Abby wondered. Suddenly the burger didn't taste so great.

"I talked to her before I left to come here," Paine said. "I promised her I would come see her at Thanksgiving."

Abby's heart sank. *Paine has a girlfriend? Wouldn't he have informed me of that?* He didn't seem like the kind of man to kiss her so passionately when there was a girlfriend somewhere.

"Is Kate your sister?" Abby asked hopefully.

Paine smiled. "No."

Abby frowned, getting angry. "Who is she, then?" She knew she sounded like a jealous lover, but she couldn't help it.

Paine reached over and covered her hand with his. Abby tried to move her hand, but Paine wouldn't let her go. "She's a good friend. About three years ago, she was being stalked." Paine removed his hand and leaned back in his chair. "Ben, Jake, and Bill helped me protect her."

Abby saw him frown. "What happened?"

"Kate had to disappear and leave our protection."

"She was gone for two years before we finally caught him," Ben said.

"It was really Kate who caught him. She set the trap, and we came in at the end to clean up," Jake said affectionately. "Jack helped her, and they caught him."

Abby was confused. "Who's Jack?"

"Her husband," Ben said. "They got married a year ago."

"We've stayed in contact with her ever since," Paine said. He thought it about it for a second. "So yes, I guess you could say she is my sister." He looked over at Ben and Jake. "She's *our* sister."

Abby refused to let Paine see how relieved she felt. "She sounds special."

"She is," Ben said. "She's invited all of us for Thanksgiving."

"Where does she live?"

"Wyoming," Jake said. "I love Kate, but Wyoming?" Jake made a funny face. "There's nothing in Wyoming but cows and buffalo."

Paine laughed. "Jake, you know you'll go, or Kate will come and get you herself."

Jake smiled. "That she would."

Abby tried to ignore the stab of jealousy she felt. It shouldn't matter to her if Paine was close to someone. She had male friends, and it didn't mean anything. She wasn't sure what bothered her more, that Paine spoke fondly of Kate or that she was actually jealous of her.

Paine started cleaning the mess off the table. "Let's all get some rest. I have a feeling it's going to be a busy day tomorrow."

Ben and Jake stood. "I'll take first watch," Ben said.

"That's good, because I can sleep in peace and won't have to listen to your snoring," Jake said.

"I don't snore, jackass," Ben said irritably.

"How do you know? You're sound asleep when you're doing it."

Ben was shaking his head in annoyance when he and Jake walked into the other room. "Well, at least I don't sing in my sleep."

Jake laughed and then stopped. "Wait, who told you that?"

Abby could hear Ben laughing when they shut the door between the two rooms.

She smiled at Paine. "Are those two safe to be in the same room?"

"They ride each other's backs a lot, but they both know they wouldn't want anyone else watching them," Paine said, smiling. "And I wouldn't want anyone else either."

Abby watched Paine continue to clean up the wrappings from their dinner. The room suddenly got very quiet. She didn't know what to do, so she just stood there.

Paine turned and looked at her. "What's the matter, Abby?"

"Nothing." She turned pink.

Paine walked over to her. "Nothing will happen unless you want it to."

Abby looked down and saw his arm. "Let's get your arm wrapped up." She went to the table and grabbed the Walgreens bag. "We should have done this before dinner. It could get infected." Abby knew she was rambling, but she couldn't seem to stop herself. "Then you definitely have to go see a doctor."

Abby felt Paine come up behind her. "Abby, I want you." He put his hands on her shoulders. Then he turned her to face him. "Do you want me?"

Abby didn't look at him but nodded. Paine lifted her chin. "Abby, I don't take making love lightly. I don't think I ever told you, but I was married for five years."

That startled Abby. "You were married?" She really didn't know anything about this man.

"We've been divorced for over three years."

"What happened?"

Paine turned and walked over to the bed. "She said I was never around. I guess I wasn't for a while." Abby watched him run his hand through his hair. She smiled. That seemed to be a habit of his. "When Kate's stalking case came into my life, I was gone a lot." He looked up at her. "I had to help her, Abby."

Abby went to Paine, knelt down in front of him, and took his hands into hers. "Why are you beating yourself up for helping someone who was in trouble? I don't know where I would be right now if it wasn't for you." Abby sat down on the bed next to him. "Frankly, I think your wife was crazy to let you go."

Paine turned and looked at her, smiling. "You do, huh?"

"Yep." Then she smiled. "But you can be a little bossy sometimes."

Paine lowered his head and started kissing her, pushing her back onto the bed. "Please tell me you want this as much as I want it."

Abby had already started taking off his shirt. "You can't tell? I must be doing something wrong."

"No, you're doing everything right." He lifted his head to look at her. "What I was trying to tell you earlier is that I want you to be in my life and not a one-night stand." Abby started to speak, but Paine stopped her. "And don't tell me it's some kind of hero thing either."

Abby went back to taking his shirt off. "I was going to tell you that you talk too much."

Paine chuckled, shrugging out of his shirt. "You're right." He started kissing her neck and her ear. Abby felt goose bumps all over her body. She reached for the button of his jeans.

"Wait." Paine started to get off the bed.

Abby held him down. "You're stopping?" She was incredulous. "I swear, Paine, if you stop now, I'm going throw you off this bed."

Paine laughed. "Honey, I'm not stopping." He got off the bed. "I'm closing the adjoining door."

Abby watched him move to the door. "Oh, good idea."

Paine shut and locked the door and started her way again. "I don't want to be interrupted."

"Yeah, me neither." Abby had a lump in her throat as she watched him. The man was too damn handsome. His chest was all skin and muscles that continued down to a flat stomach. His arms were also muscular and perfect, except for the cut on his arm. "Paine, we really should wrap your arm."

Paine stood in front of her looking down at her not saying anything.

Abby cleared her throat. "It will get infected if we don't do something about it."

Paine put both of his knees on each side of her and lay on top of her, resting on his elbows.

"Now look who's talking too much." Then he lowered his head.

*   *   *

The Black Angel watched the motel from across the street. They thought they were safe. If he wanted to, he could be in and out of there in a matter of minutes, and they would all be dead. It was the woman who was holding him back, though. She had become a challenge. She would die in the end, but right now it was more fun just to chase her. Then he thought about killing the three men and taking her. He decided he liked chasing her instead, and besides, he really didn't want to kill the men.

He knew one of the men was keeping watch. He smiled. They had no idea he was standing just a hundred yards from where they were sleeping. *Get your rest, Abby. Because before I'm done with you, you'll be scared of your own shadow.*

13

Paine woke early the next morning. He reached for his watch to see what time it was. Five o'clock. He turned and looked at the woman lying next to him. Her hair was out of its braid and spread out over her pillow. Paine couldn't help himself. He reached over and stroked her head. Abby moved and groaned but didn't wake up.

Last night had been incredible for Paine. He just hoped she felt the same, because there was no way in hell he was letting her go. He heard movement in the next room. He figured he wouldn't be able to go back to sleep, so he pushed the covers aside and walked naked into the bathroom.

After he showered and dressed, he went back into the room to check on Abby. She was still asleep, exhausted after the last two days. Paine still couldn't believe he had only known her for a couple of days. If somebody had told him he would be falling in love in just two days, he would have laughed and told them that was only in fairy tales. He couldn't deny how he felt, though. He wanted to wake her up now and tell her how much he loved her, but that would probably freak her out. Instead he went to the adjoining door and very quietly opened it and knocked on the other door.

The door opened, and Jake stood there. "Hey, boss. Couldn't sleep?"

Paine walked into the room and partially closed the door. He wanted to be able to hear what was going on in the other room.

"I slept." Paine peered out of the window and motioned. "Anything going on out there?"

"Nope. Quiet as a mouse," Jake said.

Paine kept looking out the window.

"You okay, boss?" Jake asked.

Paine still felt there was something not right about this whole situation. "I can't shake the feeling that we're missing something here."

Jake snorted. "Well, boss, we don't know anything about what's going on here."

"I know, I know," Paine said. "It's something else. How does this guy keep finding us? Do you know any drug dealer who could make a shot like the one this guy made last night?"

Jake shrugged. "I can't think of any, but that doesn't mean it can't happen." Jake went to look out the window next to Paine. "Besides you don't even know if it is a drug thing."

Paine didn't say anything.

Jake cleared his throat. "Um, it's probably not any of my business, but you like her, don't you?"

Paine's first reaction was to tell Jake he was right, it wasn't any of his business, but Jake and Ben had put their lives on the line for her. They deserved better than that.

"Yes, I do. And it scares the hell out of me."

"I think it's great, boss." Jake beamed.

Paine turned and looked at him. "I'm scared for her, Jake. This guy is not giving up, and I'm not sure what I would do without her."

"We'll just have to make sure nothing does happen to her then."

"I know. That's why I called you and Ben."

"Do you guys have any idea what time it is?" Ben said irritably.

Paine turned and looked at Ben. He was sitting up in bed, rubbing his eyes.

"Oh great," Jake said dramatically. "We woke the sleeping beast."

"Screw you, Jake." Ben got out of bed. He walked over to the coffee pot sitting on the desk and started making coffee. "What are you guys talking about, anyway?"

Paine turned away from the window and went to sit at the table. "I was telling Jake how we're missing something here."

"Like what?"

"The hell if I know," Paine said angrily. He shook his head. "I'm sorry, Ben. That's not aimed at you. I appreciate you and Jake coming to help me."

Paine could hear Abby next door. "Abby's up. Let's be ready to go in, say"—Paine looked at his watch—"an hour?"

"You got it, boss," Ben said. Paine nodded and left the room.

Jake took a chair at the table. "He likes her."

"I know," Ben said.

"You owe me a hundred dollars." Jake held out his hand, palm up.

Ben walked by and slapped his hand instead. "Not sure how you figure that."

"I bet you a hundred dollars that his change of attitude was because of a girl," Jake said patiently. "You took that bet, my friend, so now it's time to pay up."

Ben walked over to his pants on the floor and took out his wallet. Then he stopped and held it up. "How about double or nothing?"

Jake leaned forward, intrigued, resting his elbows on his knees. "What do you have in mind?"

"If Paine says thanks again in, oh, let's say the next twenty-four hours, you win."

Jake frowned. "I don't get it. That wasn't the bet."

Ben shook his head. "The bet was he said thanks because of the girl."

"Yeah, so?"

"Well, if it truly is because of the girl, then he'll say it again."

Jake thought it over then smiled. "You're on."

*   *   *

Paine stepped into the room and looked for Abby. When he saw the bed was empty his heart rate dropped, and then he heard the shower turn on. He let out a little sigh of relief. *Hell, Paine,* he thought, *she's just in the shower. You need to relax.*

He walked over to the bathroom and knocked on the door. She didn't answer. He knocked again. "Abby?"

He heard a muffled, "I'm fine. Go away."

Paine opened the door and saw Abby sitting on the floor with a sheet wrapped around her. He rushed over to her. "Abby, what's wrong, honey?" he asked, alarmed.

"Nothing. Can you just go, please?"

"Not until you tell me why you're sitting here on the floor looking as white as a ghost."

She didn't look at him.

"Abby tell me."

After a few seconds she mumbled something. "I'm sorry, honey, I didn't catch that."

"I said it's my foot. I tried taking the bandages off so I could shower, and it got stuck, and then I looked at it, and I felt like I was going to be sick. So I sat on the floor trying not to pass out."

Paine held back his laugh. He didn't think she would appreciate it right now. Instead he took her foot and examined it. "It's okay. I'll take care of it."

"I know you think it's ridiculous, but I can't help it," Abby said with her chin held high.

"I don't think it's ridiculous."

Abby looked at him, probably trying to decide if he was being sincere. "When I was a kid, my dad and I were out playing ball. I was kind of a tomboy."

She pushed a piece of hair out of her face. Paine wanted to do that for her, but instead he let her finish her story.

"I threw the ball too far, and my dad had to run and jump for it. He landed in my mom's garden on one of those green sticks that are pointy on top." She looked at him to see if he understood what she was talking about. He nodded. "It went through his arm. I freaked out and started screaming so loud that my mom came out to see what all the fuss was about." Paine saw her swallow. "There was blood everywhere. In the end, he was okay." She started to get up, so Paine helped her onto the toilet seat cover. "Anyway, since that day, I can't stand the sight of blood."

Paine got the stuck bandage off her foot. "It's only bleeding a little, Abby." He stood up. "Once you're done with your shower, I'll rebandage it for you."

Paine watched while she got up just to make sure she wasn't going to pass out.

Abby looked up at him. "I'm good now. You can go."

"I want to make sure you get in the shower okay."

"I'm fine, Paine."

He lifted her chin. "Abby, did you forget I've seen you naked?"

She turned that pretty pink again. "That's different," she croaked.

"Why?"

"Because…" She tried again. "Because—" She stopped. "You're right." Paine about fainted when she dropped the sheet and stood there in front of him.

"God, Abby." He reached for her, but she ducked out of the way.

"No way, Paine." Abby pulled the curtain aside and stepped in. "If you want to do something about it, then you're going to have to come in here with me."

Paine saw the teasing smile right before she closed the curtain. He looked at his watch and smiled. He quickly stripped down and stepped into the shower.

"Oh," he heard Abby say right before he covered her mouth with his.

*   *   *

An hour later they were sitting in a diner down the street from the sheriff's office waiting for their breakfast to arrive. It was still early, so they pretty much had the place to themselves. They sat in a booth in the back. Abby sat next to Paine, and Ben and Jake sat across from them. Paine was still reeling from the sex in the shower.

"How did you guys sleep?" Abby asked, looking at Ben and Jake.

"Well, Mr. Snorer over here," Jake said, nodding his head toward Ben. "Let's just say I didn't have to worry about falling asleep while I was on watch."

"Do you want me to tell Abby what song you sang last night?" Ben growled.

"I do not sing," Jake said to Ben and then turned to Abby. "I do not sing."

Abby laughed. "Does he have a nice voice?"

"If you like the croaking frog sound."

Jake started sputtering. "I do not sing!"

Abby and Ben both started laughing.

"Jackass," Jake said to Ben and then smiled.

The waitress arrived with their meals. "Thank you, darlin'." Jake gave the waitress a smile and a wink. She was a pretty redhead with a sprinkle of freckles across her nose. She smiled and left them to enjoy their breakfast.

"Do you have to flirt with every girl you meet?" Ben asked Jake.

"I'm just being friendly."

"Ben, have you found out anything yet?" Paine asked.

Ben gave him a strange look. "Paine, it's early. I'll have to wait until somebody gets into the precinct."

Paine knew he sounded like an ass, but he wanted to catch this guy. "Can't you call one of your computer geeks and get their ass out of bed?"

Paine could feel Abby looking at him. He turned his head to look at her.

"You're being bossy again." She scowled.

"That's because I am the boss." He scowled back. Paine knew he was making a mess of this.

"Are you always this grumpy in the morning?" Abby fired back.

Just then the bell rang on the door. "I am when there's a guy out there trying to kill you." Paine started to say something else when he noticed all the color drain from Abby's face. "Abby, what's wrong?" She was looking at the door. Paine turned to where she was staring. Ben and Jake turned to look also. A man had come in. He was built as solid as an ox, and he was bald.

The bald man was looking around, but he stopped when his eyes landed on Abby. Paine's heart stopped when he saw the man reach behind his back and take out a gun.

"Get down, Abby," he yelled. Paine threw his body over hers. Shots rang out. Their breakfast went flying everywhere. Broken dishes rained down on them. He heard Abby screaming. Ben and Jake ducked under the table and started shooting.

Paine got Abby under the table also. Paine turned to look for the man. He saw Ben and Jake overturning a table and squatted behind it. "Are you guys okay?" They both nodded. "Where is he?" Paine's heart was in his throat.

"He's behind the bar," Ben said, breathing hard.

"We have to get Abby out of here!" Paine looked around the diner. He spotted the waitress on the floor next to a table covering her ears.

"I only want girl," the bald man yelled. Paine flashed back to the night in the cabin. This was definitely the same man that started shooting at them then.

"That's not going to happen, buddy," Paine yelled back. "You're outnumbered. Why don't you give it up?"

"I only want girl," the man repeated.

Paine looked at Abby to make sure she was still safe, and then he motioned for Ben to go right and Jake to move left of the bar. They nodded and moved out from behind their cover. Paine started up the middle. Very slowly they worked their way to the bar. When Paine was in front of it, he looked at Ben and Jake to make sure they were in place. They both nodded okay to him.

At the same time they stood and yelled, "Freeze!" The man was gone.

"Go check the back," Paine ordered Ben and Jake. They took off after the man while Paine went back to Abby.

"Abby, honey, are you okay?" Paine helped her out from under the table. He grabbed a chair from a table and sat her down. "Abby?"

"I'm fine, Paine." She didn't sound fine. Her head was bowed so Paine couldn't see her face. Some of her hair had come out of the braid. He reached up and put it behind her ear, and that's when he noticed her eye.

"Abby!" he exclaimed. "Your eye." He tried to reach for her, but she stopped him.

"Don't, Paine."

"Abby, you're hurt." Paine reached for her again.

Abby put her hands on his chest to stop him. "It's okay, Paine. I hit it on the table getting down to the floor. Just go help Ben and Jake."

Paine shook his head. "I'm not leaving you, Abby."

"Then go check on that poor girl," Abby said, looking at the waitress huddled under the counter. "She's probably terrified."

Paine looked at Abby closely. He felt like she was pushing him away, and he didn't know why. Without saying anything else to her, he went to check on the waitress.

Abby watched Paine help the girl. She was crying, and he was trying to calm her down.

Paine helped her into a chair. "Here, sit. It's over now," he said in his no-nonsense voice. That just seemed to make the girl cry harder. Paine was shaking his head when he went over to the bar and grabbed a glass of water that was sitting there. He went back to the girl and handed it to her. She took it with shaky hands.

The bell rang over the door. Her heart started pounding again, and Abby couldn't help from jumping up and turning to it. To her relief, it was Ben and Jake.

"We lost him, Paine," Ben said angrily.

"There's an alley in back that leads to the main road," Jake said.

Paine left the girl, walked to Abby, and stopped in front of her. "Let's get—" They heard sirens out front, and a few seconds later the sheriff came running into the diner.

He stopped and looked at them and then the diner. "What the hell happened here, Captain?" He snarled. "You come into my town, and all hell breaks loose."

Paine took angry strides to the sheriff. "We all just about got our heads shot off, Sheriff, so why don't you back off?" Paine thundered back.

Ben stepped between the two men. "Sheriff, we could use your help here," Ben said calmly, trying to diffuse the tension.

Abby felt her body tensing as she waited to see what would happen next.

After a few seconds, the sheriff nodded. "What happened?" he said more calmly.

Abby sat back down in the chair. She didn't think her legs would hold her up for much longer. Now that the danger was over, she started shaking herself. *Well, the danger for right now,* she thought. Until they caught this guy, she knew she was still in trouble.

Paine walked back over to her and put his hand on her shoulder. It calmed Abby and her shaking lessened. "I believe we just met the guy who is trying to kill Abby." Paine looked down at Abby to confirm.

She nodded. "He's the one I saw shoot that man in the woods."

"And you lost him?" The sheriff was incredulous.

Abby felt Paine stiffen. Before he could answer, Jake stepped up. "Yeah, Sheriff, we lost him. So why don't you go see if you can find him?"

"I guess I'm going to have to do that, since you can't seem to catch him," the sheriff fired back.

"Listen, asshole—"

"You son of a bitch."

"Watch it, Sheriff."

"I didn't think you would be that incompetent," they all said at once.

Abby couldn't take it anymore. "Shut up!" she yelled once again, jumping up from the chair. They all stopped. "Just shut up!" Paine reached for her. She held up her hand to stop him. "Please," she said quietly and sat back down.

"Abby's right," Paine said, calm now. "We're going to have to work together if we're going to catch this guy."

After a moment, the sheriff nodded. "I apologize. I'm not used to this kind of stuff going on in my town."

After that, Abby tuned everything out. She couldn't think, and she didn't want to think. The diner was full of deputies and various people. Abby didn't know who they all were, and she didn't care. They left her alone, and for that she was grateful. Somebody had wrapped a blanket around her. She saw Paine looking worriedly at her every so often. Abby gave him a slight smile each time, but it only made him frown more.

She had no idea how long she sat there before Paine came up to her. "Abby?"

She looked up at him. "We're going to go over to the sheriff's office now." He bent down so he was face-to-face with her. "Are you ready to do that?"

Am I ready? What choice do I have? "Yes, Paine, I'm ready." He took her hand and helped her up. Abby headed for the door, but Paine stopped her.

"Abby, you're scaring me. What's wrong?"

"Please, Paine, let's just go."

"Not until you tell me what's wrong," he whispered, looking at the crowd in the diner. "I can't help you unless I know what's wrong."

"Nothing's wrong. Quit asking me," Abby said too loudly. People stopped and looked at her. She felt the pink start to climb up her face.

"We'll be right back," Paine said to Ben and Jake, grabbing her arm. They headed for a door down a hallway.

"What are you doing?" Abby demanded, trying to free her arm. "Let me go."

Paine didn't say anything until he had ushered them into the ladies' room. "Now, you're going to tell me what's wrong, or I swear, Abby, we'll stay here until hell freezes over." He crossed his arms and glared at her.

It was just too much. Abby burst into tears.

"Ah, hell, Abby," Paine said, and then she was in his arms. He was rubbing her back, telling her everything was going to be okay.

"You told me you thought I was strong and brave." Abby hiccupped. "I'm not. I'm scared, and right now just the thought of going outside has me shaking inside." She wiped the tears running down her face. "I don't know if I can do it, Paine." Her voice trembled.

"Abby, is that what has you upset?" Paine lifted her chin. "I do think you're strong and brave." He wiped another tear that had fallen. "It's okay to be scared. Hell, I was scared."

Abby looked at him. "You didn't look scared. You reacted. I froze just like that night at the cabin."

"I'm a cop, Abby. I'm trained to react. It's part of the job." Paine brought her in for a hug. "Abby, I'd die before I'd let anything happen to you." Abby felt him kiss the top of her head. "We're going to go outside." Abby stiffened and tried to pull away, but Paine held her tight. "We're going to cover you just like before. Only this time the sheriff will take the lead. He won't come for you, Abby, with everybody around you."

"He had no problem coming into a diner and shooting, and he didn't care who got in the way." She was trying to hold back the tears again. "He could have killed you."

Paine pulled back to look at her. "Do you trust me?"

"You know I do. It's not that."

"Then what is it?"

"I don't want you to die protecting me." Just the thought made Abby shudder.

Paine bent his head and kissed her. It was gentle and sweet. Abby leaned into him, taking it in, but she wanted more. She put her arms around his neck and deepened the kiss. She couldn't think about him dying. This time she pushed her tongue inside. Abby reached for his shirt to unbutton it, but Paine put his hands on hers, stopping her. "Honey, as much as I would like to finish this, the bathroom isn't a great place to make love."

Abby groaned and rested her forehead on his chest. "Didn't we make love in a bathroom this morning?"

Paine laughed. "You got me there."

Abby stepped away from him wiping the last of her tears. "I'm sorry. I'm ready now." She smiled. "Just had a case of female hormones."

Paine hugged her again. Someone knocked at the door. "Paine, it's Ben. Sorry man, but we really need to go."

"When this is over, you and I are going to go somewhere so we won't be interrupted." He let her go then and looked at her. "Ready?"

Abby took a deep breath. "Ready."

*   *   *

The Black Angel watched her from across the street. He wasn't worried about anyone seeing him. Everyone was focused on her. They had the woman surrounded, rushing her to a car that was parked out front. He couldn't help but smile. She thought she was safe with her entourage. He had to admit, though, that he was getting tired of this game. He needed to up the ante, and he knew exactly what to do. He gave her one last look, turned, and left.

14

Paine and Abby were sitting in the sheriff's office along with one of his deputies. Paine couldn't remember his name, but he didn't like the way he kept looking at Abby. Paine couldn't tell if it was the interest of a man in a woman, or if it was something else. He knew Abby felt it, too, because she kept fidgeting in her seat and wouldn't look at him. Paine was just getting ready to ask him what his problem was when the sheriff walked in.

"Sorry about that. Just had to take care of a problem." He sat down.

Paine got angry. "You mean more of a problem than having a killer in your town?"

Abby put her hand on Paine's knee and gave him a pointed look. Paine tried to relax.

"I still have a town to worry about, Captain."

"You should be worried about your town. This guy doesn't seem to care who gets in the way."

The sheriff leaned back. "Do you think he knew she was in that diner?"

Paine thought it over. He had been replaying the scene in his head, but everything had happened so fast that Paine couldn't be sure. The man had walked in not holding a gun. He didn't pull his gun out until he saw Abby sitting there.

"I'm not sure, Sheriff. My gut is saying no, but as I told you before, he always seems to know where we are."

"Okay, then what do you want to do?" the sheriff asked.

"We stick to the plan. We go and find the body. I still think if we can figure out who he is, then we'll have more answers."

"And what about Ms. Turner?" The sheriff looked at Abby.

"What about her? Where I go, she goes," Paine said, looking at her. She didn't seem to be too happy. He frowned at her questioningly.

"You know I'm sitting here, right?" She scowled.

The sheriff ignored her. "Fine. We should probably get started, then." The sheriff stood, and so did Paine.

"How many deputies can you spare?" Paine asked.

"I have Officer Briggs, here." The sheriff said, pointing to the man next to him. "I'm keeping the other three here to watch over the diner and the rest of the town."

"We'll take two cars. One with me, Abby, and you; and the other with Ben and Jake and your deputy here."

The deputy didn't say anything. He just gave Paine a small smile. There was just something about the deputy that rubbed Paine the wrong way, and he wanted to reach over and wipe the smile off the man's face.

"Let's head out, then."

When they were walking out of the sheriff's office, Abby pulled on his sleeve. He bent his head to hear her. "I thought Ben was going to stay here and check some things out," she whispered, looking at the sheriff walking ahead of them.

"I think we should keep him with us. The more the better," he whispered back. Paine saw the fear in her eyes. He put his arm around her waist. "It's okay, honey. We'll keep you safe."

They walked to the front where Ben and Jake were waiting. He saw Ben give Abby a smile; Jake gave her a wink. She smiled back at them. The wink didn't bother Paine this time. Abby was his, and he wasn't letting her go. He just hoped she felt the same way.

Paine turned to Ben. "Did you get what I asked?"

Ben nodded and handed the bag to Paine. He reached inside and took out two phones. Paine entered each number into the two phones and handed one to Abby. "Here, honey."

Abby took the phone and smiled. "Thanks, I've felt a little lost without one."

"They're just disposables, but they'll work until we get back home."

Paine filled Ben and Jake in on what the plan was, and then they headed out. Once outside, Paine looked around but didn't see anything out of place. They all surrounded Abby until she was in the car, and Paine quickly jumped in after her. He watched the sheriff go around to the driver's seat. He turned to look back at the car that Ben and Jake were in. The deputy drove with Jake in the front and Ben in the back.

"Where do we start?" The sheriff's question drew Paine back to his own car.

"My cabin. We'll work our way back from there." Paine gave the directions, and they were on their way.

It only took about fifteen minutes to reach his cabin. Paine didn't get out until the other car pulled up alongside them. He got out, helped Abby, and then stood, looking around. It seemed like a lifetime ago that he was here last, even though it had only been a few days. His life had changed in such a short time. He turned to the woman who had become the most important thing to him now. "You ready to do this?"

"I think so, Paine." Abby looked around. "I'm not sure if I'll be able to get us back to my car, though, but I'm willing to try."

Paine turned to Ben and Jake. "Stay close and keep your eyes open." Both men nodded. He then turned to the sheriff. "Sheriff, you take the lead with your deputy behind us," Paine ordered and was surprised when the sheriff just nodded and didn't argue.

"Okay, honey," he said to Abby. "Let's do this."

*   *   *

Abby couldn't help but sit low in the seat. If Paine noticed, he didn't say anything. After the other night, she felt exposed in the car. She tried to think of other things to keep her mind off what she was getting ready to do. She was going back into the woods. Shaking her head, she started to think about her shower this morning. Abby couldn't help smiling when she thought about Paine stepping inside the shower with her. She didn't think he would do it. Luckily for her, she was pleasantly surprised. Just the thought of what they did got her all hot and bothered. Maybe she shouldn't think about that, either.

Abby was still trying to think of some safe topic when she heard Paine say, "We're here."

She tried to ignore the tremors running through body because she was about to enter the woods where she had run for her life. In spite of what she told Paine, she didn't know if she could even try. She took a deep breath and climbed out of the car. Paine followed and soon they were all gathered in a huddle, looking around.

"Okay, Abby. Which way?" the sheriff asked.

"Over there." She pointed in the direction of some fallen branches. Abby still wasn't sure, but that direction made the most sense. That night she had approached Paine's cabin from the front.

"Okay, let's go," Paine said.

Her steps faltered, but then she felt Paine step next to her, lightly touching her back. He always seemed to know when she needed him. Just that slight touch gave her the courage to move on.

They had been walking for about fifteen minutes when Abby recognized where she had fallen and hit her head. "This is where I fell." She pointed to the tree stump. Abby watched Paine bend down and look at it.

"Are you sure, Abby?"

"I'm sure, Paine," she said defensively. "Look." She pointed through the trees where they'd come from.

Paine stood to look. "What? I don't see anything."

"If you look very closely, you can just make out your cabin."

They all turned and looked closer. "Remember, it was dark, and you had your lights shining. That's how I found you," she said triumphantly.

Paine turned and smiled at her. "That's good, Abby. Which direction were you coming from?"

She thought back to that night and remembered being smacked in the face by tree branches before she saw Paine's house. Abby looked around and spotted a cluster of trees. "This way." She started in that direction, but Paine stopped her.

"Abby, you have to wait for me."

In her excitement, she'd forgotten. "Right."

Paine stepped ahead of her and went in the direction she had pointed to earlier. Once there, they stopped.

"Now this is where I'm fuzzy," Abby said, biting her lip. "I had been running about twenty minutes before I ran into these branches. It started raining hard, and I couldn't see very far in front of me."

Abby was frustrated that she couldn't remember everything from that night. Then an idea occurred to her. She turned to the sheriff. "Is there a road of some kind near here?"

The sheriff thought about it. "Not really."

Abby's heart sank.

"Wait," the sheriff said. "There is an old road that leads to a beach that hardly gets used anymore because the riptide is too strong there. We don't advertise it, and only locals really know about the beach."

"Which way?" Abby was trying not to get excited, but she was sure it was going to be the right road.

The sheriff pointed to the left. "That way."

They all headed out in that direction, and within ten minutes of walking, they hit the road. Abby looked in both directions, looking for her car.

"Damn it," she said, frustrated. "I don't see my car."

Paine came up next to her. "You're doing great, Abby." She saw him looking both ways also. "What's your gut telling you, Abby? Which way?"

Abby knew she had been on the road for at least fifteen minutes before her car died. "Sheriff, how far back is the main road?"

"Oh, I don't know. Maybe ten minutes?"

"Then we need to go that way." Abby pointed to the left. Once again they all moved as a group heading in the direction of the beach. *I hope this is right,* Abby thought. She really didn't want to backtrack again. Her foot was feeling better, but just this little excursion was making it sore.

Abby looked around at her surroundings, but nothing was looking familiar. It had been dark, and she'd really hadn't paid attention. She kept looking straight ahead at the road, hoping for some sign that she was on the right track. Occasionally Abby would look on each side of the road hoping to recognize something, but she didn't think she would remember one tree from the other.

They had just walked around a bend when Abby saw her car. "Look!" Without thinking, Abby started running for it. She never thought she would be so happy to see her old car. Paine yelled something behind her, but she ignored him. When she reached her car, she was out of breath but smiling and happy. *I did it.* Then she saw Paine's face, and her smile turned into a frown.

"Damn it, Abby. What were you thinking?"

She glared at him. "I was thinking, 'Yay, I found my car!'"

Paine grabbed her arm. "You can't be that stupid."

Abby could feel the heat climb up her face. Embarrassed, she looked at the men standing behind Paine, who were trying to look anywhere except at them.

She jerked her arm out of Paine's hand. "I am not stupid," she shot back. "I just got excited that I found my car!"

Paine tried to reach for her, but she turned away. "Abby, I'm sorry."

"Don't worry about it, Paine." She started walking again, fighting off tears. She refused to embarrass herself by crying. "It's not too far from here," she said to no one in particular.

Paine caught up to her. "I'm sorry, Abby. I was out of line," he whispered. "I was just worried."

"I said it's okay, Paine. Just forget it." Abby was still stinging from his "stupid" remark and couldn't look at him. To her relief, he let it go.

Abby started to walk slower when she saw an opening in the trees. *Could this be the place?* She stopped and looked around. She had been able to see her car when she went into the trees.

"What is it, honey?" Paine asked.

"I think this is it."

Paine motioned for the rest of the group to catch up. "Okay, we're going in here." He turned to Abby. "We're right behind you, honey."

Abby nodded and started into the trees.

15

Paine was calling himself all sorts of names. *How could I have yelled at her like that?* It didn't matter that his heart about fell out of his chest when she had taken off running. All he could think about was that the shooter was out there waiting for her. He was going to have to make it up to her. She'd told him it was okay, but somehow Paine didn't think it was going to be that easy. Lost in thought, he almost ran into Abby when she suddenly stopped.

Paine looked over her shoulder and saw a body lying on the ground in an open area of trees. He stepped around her and motioned for Ben to stay with her. Ben nodded and stepped to the left of her.

Paine slowly made his way to the body, still looking around. He didn't think the killer would be here, but it didn't stop Paine from taking out his gun. Jake and the sheriff were walking next to him, with the deputy trailing slightly behind.

When they reached the body, they all stood looking down at him. He was tall and thin, and except for his face being white and the bullet hole in his chest, he looked like he could just have been lying there sleeping. "Do you know him, Sheriff?" Paine asked.

"No, I've never seen him, but that doesn't mean he's not from around here."

Paine looked around the area. "Let's spread out and see what we can find." He looked over at Abby. She was standing there looking frightened. Paine couldn't stand seeing her like that, so he walked over to her. Ben stepped aside. Paine took her hands. "Abby, are you okay?"

She nodded. "I was starting to think that maybe it wasn't real, but seeing him lying there, it just brings back that night."

Paine could feel her shivering. He wrapped his arms around her. "I know I keep saying this, but everything is going to be okay."

After a few moments, Abby pushed on his chest. "I know it is, Paine," she said, stepping out of his arms. "I'm fine now. Go do whatever it is you need to do."

Paine felt the rejection, and it stung. He knew he deserved it, but he couldn't leave with her still mad at him. "Abby." He started for her but heard Jake calling his name.

"Paine, you better come and take a look at this."

Frustrated that he couldn't finish his conversation with Abby, he gave her one last look, turned, and started walking to where Jake was standing. The sheriff and the deputy were standing next to him. Paine could feel Abby and Ben behind him. His whole body stiffened when he saw what they were looking at. It was another body.

Paine heard Abby gasp behind him. She stepped next to him.

"It's him," she whispered. "I don't understand. It's the bald guy. That's the guy who shot the other man."

Paine turned to her and put his arm around her waist. "It's okay, Abby." He felt like a broken record. In actuality, he had no idea what was going on, and it was starting to bother the hell out of him.

"I don't understand," Abby said again.

"Sheriff, you better get some help out here." Paine turned to Abby and pointed. "Honey, why don't you go sit on that tree stump over there."

"I'm fine, Paine. I don't need you to dismiss me like some kind of child."

Paine let out a frustrated breath. "I'm not dismissing you, Abby. This is going to take a while, and I noticed you're starting to limp."

He saw her turning pink again. She really was quite charming.

"Oh. Okay."

Without saying anything else, she went and sat on the stump. He turned to Ben. "Keep an eye on her," he whispered.

"You know I will, boss."

After that things were chaotic. The sheriff had called in reinforcements, but Paine felt like the whole town had decided to show up. It was probably the most excitement this town had ever had. Two dead bodies in one week had to be a record.

Paine was just getting ready to yell at some uniform for stepping on the crime scene when Ben walked up to him and lowered his voice. "Paine, I just got a call from my friend running the search on the sheriff and his father."

"And?" Paine asked impatiently.

"He couldn't find anything abnormal." Ben turned to see where the sheriff was. "The asshole father made his money from lingerie." Ben smiled. "Have you ever heard of Now You See It?"

Paine nodded. "Yeah, my ex loved that store."

"Well, that's him. It's public record, but the father tends to keep it on the down-low." Ben chuckled. "Apparently, he's embarrassed because he was the original designer. He put his wife down as president when he started the company twenty years ago, but she has since died. He still runs the company but doesn't design anymore."

"Okay, what about the son?"

"Nothing there, either. He went to a university in Seattle, and after he graduated—with pretty good grades, I might add—he came back here, and with his father's help, ran for sheriff."

Paine ran his hand through his hair. "Damn it. I thought for sure there was something off with the father and sheriff."

"Being an asshole doesn't make you a criminal," Ben said.

"I still think there's something going on in this town, and whether the sheriff knows about it or not, we need to find out what it is." Paine looked at Abby. "I don't think Abby will be safe until we do."

Paine and Ben looked at Abby, and saw her yawning. "Why don't I take her back to the motel? With the bald guy dead, the danger should be gone. And besides, you're still going to be here awhile, and it's getting dark."

Paine started to protest, but Ben interrupted. "I'll take Deputy Briggs with me."

Paine shook his head. "You're probably right, but I want to make sure, and I think she'll be safer here with me."

"Paine, I'll protect her with my life."

Paine looked at him. "I know you would, Ben, and I didn't mean any disrespect." Paine looked to Abby again. "She means everything to me, and it scares the hell out of me."

Ben smiled and slapped him on the shoulder. "Congratulations, boss, it sounds like you're in love."

Paine scowled at Ben. "I know that. I just don't know what to do about it."

Paine thought it through. He also thought the danger had passed. With the bald guy dead, Abby had no other knowledge of what was going on that night. Paine looked at her. She did look as if she were about ready to drop. *Could I let her out of my sight?* He'd been at her side for the last two days. He didn't know if he could let her go. He watched her cover her mouth and yawn again.

He turned to Ben. "Okay. Take the deputy and call me as soon as you get to the motel." They both started walking to Abby. "Don't let her out of your sight. I don't care if she has to use the restroom—you go in there with her."

Ben grinned. "I'll let you tell her that."

Paine grinned back at him, remembering the time in the woods. "Okay, maybe you don't have to go in there with her, but stay close." Then he thought about it. "Oh, and remember to cover your ears."

Ben looked at him as if he'd lost his mind. Maybe he had for letting her out of his sight. Paine trusted Ben to protect her, but truth be told, he just didn't want her to go.

Abby watched Paine and Ben walking toward her. She knew something was up, and it had her nerves on edge. *Now what?*

When they were in front of her, Paine bent down to her. "Honey, Ben's going to take you back to the motel."

Abby's heart started pounding. "Shouldn't I stay here with you?" She hated how pathetic she sounded, but she was scared to leave Paine.

He took one of her hands into his. "Abby, you're about ready to collapse, and I'm going to be a while yet."

Abby looked around at the activity going on. They had already been at it for hours, and it didn't seem to be slowing down. She looked at Paine again. "I'm really okay, Paine. I don't mind waiting."

"Abby, you go with Ben, and you need to listen to what he says," Paine said firmly.

Abby stiffened at his words. She stood up with Paine following her. "I'll go," she said without looking at him. Instead, she looked to Ben. "You ready?"

Ben looked back and forth at her and Paine. "Um, sure. Let's go." He bent his arm and waited for her to take it.

Abby took it, and they started walking. "Big jerk," she mumbled.

Ben looked down at her. "Sometimes I would agree with that statement, but this time I think he's just worried about you, Abby."

She snorted. "He has a funny way of showing of it."

"Give him a break, Abby. It was my idea, and it's killing him to let you leave."

Abby wanted to be mad at Paine. She didn't want to leave him, but she was tired of this whole mess, *and* it annoyed her that Paine was right. She was tired and hungry, and she seemed to be taking it out on him. Paine had a job to do, and it would probably be easier for him if she weren't around. Damn it, now she felt bad. Abby turned and looked for him. He was still standing there, watching her. She gave him a small smile and wave. He grinned back at her.

They reached the car. Abby hadn't even realized that Deputy Briggs had been following them. She had been too busy thinking about Paine and what she was going to do after this was all over. He had told her he wanted to keep seeing her, but she was afraid that after the danger was gone and she didn't need his protection any longer, Paine might change his mind. Abby didn't think she could count her feelings as the hero-worship thing anymore. She wanted Paine in her life. She was getting a headache trying to figure it all out.

"Abby, you and I are going in the backseat, and the deputy can drive," Ben said, opening the back door for her.

Abby got in and slid over to make room for Ben. She watched as the deputy got behind the wheel. When they were on the road, she turned to Ben. "What do you think happened back there? Who killed the bald man?"

Ben shrugged. "I don't know, Abby. Maybe his partner in crime, and it's just another asshole we're going to have to find."

"Don't you get tired?" she asked.

Ben looked at her questioningly. "What do you mean?"

"It seems like a never-ending job. There's always somebody else you have to catch."

"We call it job security," Ben said teasingly.

Abby punched him in the arm. "You know what I meant."

Ben turned serious. "I know what you meant, Abby. But what do we do? Just give up and let them take over?"

"No, I suppose you wouldn't do that."

Ben smiled and looked at the deputy up front. "What do you think, Deputy Briggs? Do we just give up?"

Abby saw the man smile in the rearview mirror. "No, we can't give up. And please just call me Henry. Or Hank if you prefer."

Abby froze. Her heart started pounding out of her chest. *It couldn't be. There were lots of Hanks out there, right?*

she reasoned with herself. What if he was the same Hank the dead man was talking about?

Abby looked at the deputy in the mirror and knew it was him. She must have given something away, because he gave her a mocking smile.

Abby looked at Ben. He was staring ahead, unaware of anything going on. She reached over to touch his hand, trying not to draw attention. "I wouldn't if I was you." The deputy said in a deadly voice.

Before Abby could do anything, the deputy had the car pulled over to the side of the road. Ben looked at him. "What are you—" Ben stopped when he saw the gun.

"Sorry, Detective, but I think Abby here just figured something out." He turned the gun on Abby. "Didn't you, bitch?"

Abby couldn't answer because she was numb with fear. She watched as the man turned his gun on Ben. "Very slowly, take out your gun."

Ben reached behind his back and pulled his gun out. The deputy reached down by his side and the back window started to roll down. "Throw it out."

Ben hesitated.

"Do it now, or I swear I'll shoot her," he said once again, pointing the gun at her.

Ben tossed the gun out and glared at the deputy. "You're a cop. How can you do this?"

"Like the lady said, it's an endless job."

Ben snorted. "Or more likely, it has to do with money."

"That's right. I like the money," he said without any guilt. "Now I want you to get out and come around to the driver's side. And don't try anything funny, because I have no problem killing her."

Ben looked at her and smiled. "Don't worry, Abby. It's going to be okay."

The man laughed. "That's very touching, but move your ass now!"

Abby kept her eye on the deputy. He was watching Ben move around the car. He never turned his back on her as he scooted over to the passenger side. Abby laughed to herself. *Right, like if I had a chance, I would have taken him?*

Ben got in the driver's seat. The deputy sat facing Ben, but he could still see Abby. "Okay, this is how it's going to work." The man actually smiled. "You just keep driving and do what I say, and everything will be fine."

"You're not going to let us live, so why don't you just do it here and get it over with?" Ben snarled.

"Because it won't be long before your friends come this way, and I need a head start." He turned to Abby. "They'll be too busy looking for you two. Meanwhile, I'll be out of the country before they even realize I had anything to do with it."

"I like how you think you're going to be able to leave the country." Ben started the car and pulled out onto the road.

"I've been keeping my eye on you," the deputy said to Abby. "I wondered if that idiot Ted had said anything that night." He smiled coldly. "And clearly he did."

"I don't know anything," Abby lied.

The deputy laughed. "As soon as I said my name, I could see it on your face." He turned to Ben. "I sent Ivan to you this morning." He shook his head. "The stupid Russian couldn't even get that right."

"So you took care of him yourself," Ben said.

The deputy smiled. "It helps me that he's dead."

Abby didn't know what to do. He was going to kill them and leave them—who knew where? She could already see Paine blaming himself. She had to think of something.

Abby looked at Ben in the mirror. She tensed up when she realized Ben was trying to tell her something. He kept looking at her seat belt and nodding his head slightly toward the deputy. At first Abby couldn't figure out what he was trying to tell her, and then she knew. She shook her head, frowning back at Ben. He smiled at her, and then he turned to the deputy.

"So you might as well tell us what's going on. It's drugs, right?"

The deputy didn't say anything.

"Since you're this close to Canada, you probably don't have any trouble getting them to the United States. Especially since you're a cop. Nobody would question it."

Abby could feel the car picking up speed. *Don't do this, Ben!* she screamed in her head.

"Hey, slow down," the deputy yelled. Ben pressed the gas harder. "Slow down now!"

"No way, asshole." Ben looked in the mirror at Abby. "Now!"

Abby grabbed onto the back of the seat and tried to brace herself. Ben turned the wheel sharply to the left and the car went over the side. The car bounced down the side of the mountain. She had a death grip on the back of the seat trying not to get jostled around. She didn't know how long they had gone before Abby saw the cliff. "Ben," she screamed. Ben tried to stop but it was too late. At first it felt to Abby as if they were flying. She felt weightless, but the feeling didn't last long. They hit the ground so hard her teeth rattled, and then they slammed into a tree. Her seat belt locked and held her back so firmly she felt her breath leave her. Abby closed her eyes trying to catch her breath. Her chest hurt, and her head didn't feel much better. *But I'm alive.* Then she remembered Ben. He hadn't been wearing his seat belt.

"Ben?" She choked and coughed.

Abby tried to undo her belt, but it was stuck. She was still trying to get it loose when she saw the deputy move. Heart racing, Abby stopped and watched him. He was bleeding from his head, and she could see blood on the windshield. She held back her gag reflex. He was groaning, but she didn't think he was conscious. She quickly tried to undo her belt again, but it wouldn't budge. She heard Ben moaning. Abby yanked on the belt again, and she still couldn't get it loose. She screamed in frustration, yanked with all her strength, and the belt came loose. She was momentarily stunned but heard the deputy groan again, and that galvanized her into action.

She opened her door and very slowly got out. She tried to ignore the pain in her chest and went to Ben's door. He was also bleeding from his head, but he wasn't moving. The airbag had gone off, and he was slumped over the steering wheel. Abby shook him, her heart in her throat. *Please, God, don't let him be dead*, she silently prayed. She let out a breath of relief when he stirred. "Ben, can you hear me?"

"Well, that was fun," he murmured.

Abby laughed. "I would expect that answer from Jake, but not you."

"I think he's rubbing off on me." He laughed and then groaned. "Ow, that hurts."

"How bad is it, Ben? We need to get out of here," Abby said, glancing at the deputy. She was thankful to see he was still not moving.

"It's not bad, Abby. I think I might have broken a rib or two, though."

"I was trying to tell you it wasn't a good idea," she scolded. "Can you move?"

"Don't worry about me. You go and get some help."

"I'm not leaving you alone with this guy, so you might as well get your ass moving out of this damn car."

Ben grinned. "You're almost as bossy as Paine."

She glared at him. "We'll discuss that later, but right now, let's get you out of here."

It took all of Abby's strength, and Ben did what he could, but with his injuries, it was slow and painful for him. Eventually they got him out of the car. Abby was breathing hard. She had her arm around his waist, and his was over her shoulder.

"Okay, I think we should head in the direction of—and I can't believe I'm going to say this—the trees," she said between breaths. It was dark again, and the trees were making the same noise as the other night. She knew it was only the wind, but it was creepy.

"That's a good idea, Abby. When he wakes up, he'll think we're headed for the road." They started to move, but Ben stopped her. "Do you see his gun anywhere?"

Letting go of Ben, Abby made sure the deputy was still unconscious before she looked around for the gun. "I don't see it, Ben." The deputy moaned. "And I don't think we have the time to keep looking," she said urgently.

"Okay, then, let's go."

They started off. It was even slower going than before, because Ben was in pain, and he was too heavy for her to carry. They had to stop several times so Abby could catch her breath. Her chest was sore, and her whole body was starting to ache. She turned her head suddenly when she heard a noise coming from the direction of the car.

"We need to hide, Ben." She looked around, trying to find a hiding spot. It was blessing and a curse that the moon was shining brightly. It helped for escaping, but it also meant that the deputy would be able to see them.

Ben looked up and pointed. "Over there by that clump of trees."

Abby looked in the direction he indicated. It was another hidey-hole like the one she'd hidden in the other night. "Okay, let's go."

Ben was starting to lose consciousness. "Stay with me, Ben," she said desperately. Abby ended up dragging him the last few feet. She sat him up, trying to get him over the fallen tree. "Ben, you have to help me!"

"Just go, Abby. Call Paine when you're far enough ahead."

The phone! Abby forgot about the phone. She had put it in her pocket when Paine had given it to her earlier. *I can call Paine! She hoped there was cell service.* But she wasn't leaving Ben out in the open.

"I will call Paine, and I'll tell him how I couldn't leave you here because you were so wimpy you couldn't even crawl over a damn tree branch."

Ben chuckled and then coughed. "Okay, I'm moving." He got up, groaning, but with Abby's help, they got him inside the hole.

"Okay, move over," Abby ordered.

"You were going to go for help."

"I'm not leaving, and before you start arguing, it's not for you. I don't want to be in the woods again, alone in the dark and running. So scoot over."

Abby could hear Ben moving, but his breathing was starting to worry her. He was taking short shallow breaths, and it sounded like he was wheezing. "Are you okay, Ben?"

"I'm fine, Abby. Just call Paine and get us the hell out of here," Ben said between gasps.

In the tight quarters, it was hard for Abby to get her phone out of her pocket. After a few tries, it finally came loose. She pressed the button and was looking for the number Paine had programmed into it. Abby found the number and hit the call button.

It seemed to take forever for Paine to answer, but on the third ring he did. "Hi, honey. You guys at the motel?"

"Paine," she whispered. "We're in trouble."

"What's wrong, Abby?" Paine asked urgently. "Where are you?"

"It's the deputy." Abby stopped when she heard a noise.

"Abby, where are you?" She could hear Paine yelling in the phone, but Abby swore she heard footsteps.

"Turn off the phone," Ben said quietly. "It's too bright."

Abby hit the off button and listened as the footsteps got closer.

16

Paine was still yelling into the phone when Jake and the sheriff came over. "What's wrong, boss?" Jake asked.

Paine ran a hand through his hair. "It was Abby," he choked out. "She said that she and Ben were in trouble."

He started running for the car, with Jake and the sheriff following. Paine called Abby's phone, but she didn't answer. He tried again and wanted to scream when she didn't answer.

"Where are they?" Jake asked anxiously.

"I don't know. She hung up." Paine prayed that she had hung up the phone on her own and that somebody hadn't done it for her. "I have to find her." Paine's heart was in his throat. He knew he shouldn't have let her leave. He reached the car and started for the driver's side.

"I'll drive, Paine," Jake said. Paine nodded and headed around the car for the passenger's door. That's when he noticed the sheriff getting ready to get in the backseat. His anger took over. Paine grabbed the sheriff and pushed him against the car. "Where is she?"

"I don't know what you're talking about." The sheriff barked out, trying to get Paine's hands off him. "Let go of me, right now!"

Paine shook him harder. "Abby said it was the deputy."

"Paine, let him go." Jake tried to peel him off the sheriff.

Paine ignored him. "Where are they?" He asked again.

"I don't know. I swear to you I have no idea what's going on!" the sheriff yelled.

"Paine, damn it, let him go. We're wasting time."

The words penetrated Paine's head. Jake was right; they were wasting time, but where did they start to look?

He let go of the sheriff and turned to Jake. "Get in, and let's head down the road." Paine didn't know what else to do. He'd never felt so hopeless in his life. Abby was out there somewhere, waiting for him to come to her. Paine wanted to smash something in frustration; he had no idea where to look.

Paine had just gotten in the car when his phone rang again. "Abby!"

"Paine, we need help." He could barely hear her.

"Honey, tell me where you are, and I'll come."

"We crashed, and Ben's hurt."

Paine tried to keep calm. "Where are you, Abby?"

"We're just up the road. Ben crashed us intentionally so we could get away from the deputy."

Paine motioned for Jake to start driving. "We're coming, Abby. Just hang on."

"He's here, Paine." Then the phone went dead.

Abby clicked the phone off and turned to Ben. It was hard to see him in the dark, but she didn't think he was conscious anymore. She could hear him breathing, though, and felt relieved, but she had other things to worry about. The deputy had passed them once, but now he was back.

If they could stay hidden until Paine got here, they just might make it out of there alive.

Abby tensed up when she heard Ben moan. Her instinct was to cover his mouth, but he was already having trouble breathing, and she didn't want to make it worse.

Abby turned her head to look out of their hiding spot. She could see the deputy just a few feet away. Did he hear Ben? The deputy had stopped and was looking around.

"I know you're here, so you might as well come out."

Abby didn't say anything. The deputy's words were slurred as if he'd been drinking. *He must be hurt,* Abby thought.

She let out a breath when he started to walk away, and that's when Ben moaned again. The deputy stopped and turned to their hiding spot. He slowly made his way over. She started to panic. *What do I do? We're like sitting ducks here.* She watched him coming closer, and then he stopped in front of her.

"Come out here, now!" he demanded.

Abby tried to think. *He'll kill us if we come out, but I can't do anything from here.* She decided her best chance was outside and in the open. She looked again at Ben and then started climbing out of their hiding spot.

When she was out, she turned and looked at the deputy. He didn't look so good. Maybe they had a chance, but he was holding a gun on her.

"You've been nothing but trouble," he snarled. Blood was dripping down his face and into his eyes. He reached up and wiped it away. "It is going to give me the greatest pleasure to kill you," he said, spitting blood out of his mouth.

Abby felt as if she were about to throw up. There was just too much blood.

"But first," he said, "I need to take care of your friend." He was motioning with his gun for her to move.

Abby moved to the left. "He's hurt."

The deputy's bloodstained teeth showed through his smile. "Then I guess killing him won't matter."

Abby looked around for anything she could use as a weapon. She spied a broken tree limb just to the left of her. *Can I get to it?* Her heart thumped against her chest. *You can do this, Abby! Do it for Paine! Do it for Ben!* She slowly inched her way over, keeping an eye on the deputy.

He wasn't looking at her, instead focusing on their hiding spot. "Come out of there, asshole."

Ben didn't answer.

She moved a little closer. Almost there!

The deputy cocked his gun, and all hell broke loose. Ben growled and threw something at the deputy's face. *Do it now, Abby!* She lunged for the tree limb and in one motion ran for the deputy and swung. Abby heard a crunch, but the deputy was still standing. She swung again. This time he deflected the blow, and the tree limb flew out of Abby's hands. He turned toward her, raising the gun. It seemed like everything was in slow motion, and then Abby found herself looking down the barrel of the gun.

"You bitch!"

"I love you, Paine," Abby whispered, closing her eyes and waiting for the bullet to hit her.

She screamed when the shot rang out. But where was the pain? She opened her eyes to see a surprised expression cover the deputy's face before he fell to the ground.

Abby turned and saw Paine. He was standing there holding the gun out in front of him. *Paine was here!* She tried to walk to him but made the mistake of looking down at the deputy. His eyes were still open, and he had a bullet hole in his forehead. It was just too much. She threw up.

Paine ran over to Abby, his heart pounding. He had almost been too late. The asshole had had his gun pointed at her, and he'd just reacted. He barely glanced at the man lying on the ground with his head blown open. All he could think about was getting to Abby. When he reached her she was on her knees wiping her hand across her mouth.

"You okay, honey?" He put his hand on her back.

Abby looked up at him. "I'm fine." She turned and looked at the deputy and immediately threw up again. Paine stayed with her, holding her hair out of the way.

When she was done, he helped her up and moved her away from the body. "Ben, you have to help Ben," he heard her say.

"Where is he, honey?"

She pointed to a cluster of trees.

Paine could hear sirens and men shouting. They were about to be bombarded. "Jake!" he yelled over the noise. Jake stopped examining the deputy's body and looked at Paine. "Ben's in that clump of trees there."

Jake nodded and ran over there.

"I'm sorry I threw up," Abby whispered looking up at him. "I probably contaminated the crime scene."

He hid his smile. "It's okay, honey. When I saw the deputy holding his gun on you, I felt a little sick myself." What he had really felt was rage.

"Really?" Abby asked doubtfully.

He smiled. "I swear." Then his smiled faded. "I was afraid I was going to be too late." He swallowed the lump in his throat. "I don't know, Abby, what I would have done."

"But you weren't too late." She took his hand. "In fact, I'd say you were just in time."

Paine looked at her beautiful smile and couldn't stop himself. He put his arms around her and squeezed tightly. He just wanted to hold her and never let go, but then he heard her cry of pain. Paine immediately pulled back. "What's wrong, Abby? Are you hurt?"

She had her hand on her chest. "It's nothing, Paine. My chest hurts a little from the seat belt."

"We need to get you to the hospital."

Abby started moving to where Ben was hiding. "It's not me who needs the hospital."

Paine followed her just to make sure she wasn't going to fall down. He smiled when he heard Jake talking.

"I'm telling you right now, it's not going to be me who has to explain about the car to the rental agency."

"Would you just shut up and help me out of here?" Ben growled.

"Well, since you asked me so nicely," Jake said sarcastically.

Abby started to bend down to help, but Paine stopped her. "Honey, I'll do it."

He went to help Jake and saw Ben for the first time. His face was covered in dirt and blood. He was holding his ribs, and his breathing didn't sound good.

"So you crashed the car, huh?" Paine asked, pulling him out of the hole.

"Sorry, boss. It's all I could think of at the time," Ben said through a groan.

With Paine helping, it didn't take long to get Ben out. They sat him down and leaned him against a tree. His breathing was getting shallower. Jake looked at Paine with concern. "Hang in there, Ben, we'll get you to the hospital."

"I'm okay, Paine. How's Abby?" Ben said, looking around for her.

Smiling, Abby squatted down. "I'm fine, Ben. You saved us."

Ben tried to laugh but started coughing instead. When he was finished, he turned to her. "I just got us out of the car. You saved us." Then he turned to look at Paine. "I told her to go for help, but she wouldn't listen."

Paine turned and looked at Abby. "Yeah, sometimes she's not good at that," he said, reaching for her hand and kissing the back of it.

Abby smiled and then shrugged. Paine chuckled and turned back to Ben. "Thank you, Ben," he said seriously.

Ben tried to shrug it off. "It was nothing."

Paine touched his shoulder. "No, Ben. Thank you."

Ben looked back him. After a hesitation, Ben nodded.

They all jumped when Jake hollered. "Hah, I'll collect my two hundred bucks later, Ben."

Paine looked at Jake, frowning. "What the hell are you talking about, Jake?"

"Nothing, boss. Just a little side wager between Ben and me."

Paine had started to ask about the wager when the sheriff walked up. "The paramedics are here."

Paine stood and turned to the sheriff. "No offense, Sheriff, but I don't trust anyone in your department."

The sheriff shook his head. "None taken. I don't either."

Paine might have almost felt sorry for the man if it hadn't been for almost losing Abby. And Ben.

"The FBI will probably be taking over now. I have a feeling your whole department is going to be taken apart and scrutinized."

"I know," the sheriff said dejectedly.

After that, things moved pretty quickly. The paramedics took Ben and, after some arguing, Abby to the hospital. Abby kept telling Paine she was fine, but he knew he would feel better when she had been checked over.

Paine and Jake followed them to the hospital while the sheriff took care of the crime scene. Paine had a feeling it would be the last thing the sheriff was in charge of for a while.

Now Paine and Jake were sitting out in the waiting area. It was a small room with chairs scattered around. Paine never understood why they never put more comfortable chairs in waiting rooms. These chairs were made out of wood with very thin padding on the seats. The room was empty except for Paine and Jake. He felt like his nerves were about to explode. He knew Abby was okay, but the waiting was driving him nuts.

"Paine, she's fine," Jake said.

"I know, Jake." He stood. "It was just too damn close. If we had been even a minute longer, both she and Ben would probably be dead."

Jake stood, too. "But we weren't, Paine. And they're both going to be okay."

Just then the doctor walked in. "Who's Paine?"

Paine stepped up. "That's me. How's Abby?"

"She's going to be fine. She has a mild concussion and some sore muscles."

Paine turned his head and smiled at Jake.

"We are going to keep her here for the night, though."

Paine turned to look at the doctor, frowning. "Why, if she's okay?"

"It's just a precaution. She'll get to go home in the morning." Paine let out a breath. *She's fine.*

"What about Ben?" Jake asked.

"He wasn't quite as lucky as Ms. Turner. He has a couple of broken ribs, a broken wrist, and a concussion. He's going to be sore as hell. He'll have to stay for a couple of days at least."

"When can we see them?" Paine asked.

"They're just getting them to their rooms. Once they're settled you can go in and see them."

"Thank you, Doctor," Paine said, shaking his hand.

"You're welcome." The doctor smiled and left.

Paine sat back down in his chair. *Abby's going to be okay, and it's over. I'm happy she's out of danger, but now what?* he thought. *Will she still want to be with me?*

Paine was sure what they had was special, but did she feel the same? They had only known each other for a few days, but what they had been through together made it seem longer.

"What's wrong, boss? She's going to be fine," Jake said.

Paine shook his head. "Nothing, Jake. I'm just glad it's over."

Jake laughed. "She's a feisty one, that's for sure."

Paine smiled. He couldn't argue with that.

"Ben told me while they were working on him out there that she practically dragged him into the woods."

Paine nodded absently.

"So if you're not going to go for it, do you mind if I give it a try?"

Paine turned to Jake when it finally dawned on him what he said. "Don't even think about it, Jake," Paine snarled.

"So does that mean you're going to go for it?" Jake asked, grinning.

Paine smiled when he realized Jake was teasing him. "Yeah, it means I'm going to go for it."

"Well, hot damn, Paine." Jake slapped him on the back.

Paine laughed. He knew he would do whatever it took to keep Abby in his life. When they got back to Portland, he would take her out and see where it led.

Paine looked up when a tall elderly nurse came in. "They're both in their rooms now. If you want I can show you the way." The nurse turned without waiting for an answer.

Paine and Jake stood and followed her down the hall.

"I hate hospitals," Jake whispered.

"Why?"

"They're always full of sick people."

Paine laughed, shaking his head. The nurse had stopped in front of a door when they caught up to her. "Mr. Jones is in this room," she said, pointing to the door she was standing in front of. "And Ms. Turner is across the hall." She pointed across the hall.

Paine thanked the nurse; she smiled and left.

"You go see Abby. I'll check up on Mr. Snorer in here."

"I can hear you, jackass," Paine heard Ben say from inside his room.

"Jeez, don't get so testy." Jake winked at Paine, and then he entered the room.

"I don't get testy," Ben said testily. Paine smiled and headed to Abby's room.

When he walked in, she was sitting up with the sheets pulled up around her. Her hair was loose and framing her face. She didn't notice him, so he stood there just staring at her. She was beautiful, and Paine couldn't help smiling when she kept moving the bed up and then down. "Damn bed," she muttered.

"You're going to break it if you keep messing with it," Paine joked and walked the rest of the way in.

Abby looked up at him and then turned pink. "I think it's already broken. It's like it has a mind of its own." She kept messing with the controls.

"Where do you want it?" Paine asked, taking the bed remote from her.

"I don't know," she said, blowing her hair of her eyes. "This has to be the most uncomfortable bed I've ever been in."

"Even more than the one in the cabin that first night?" Paine asked, watching her reaction.

She looked up at him and smiled shyly. "That one would have been perfect except for the crazy man chasing us."

Paine's heart started racing. He looked into her eyes and knew that she wanted him as much as he wanted her. He slowly lowered his head and kissed her. Paine felt her hand go around his neck. He tasted peppermint. Abby was pulling him down on top of her, but Paine knew this wasn't the place to start something they couldn't finish.

"Honey, as much as I want to continue this, somebody could walk in at any time," he said gently, pulling her hands away, breathing hard.

"So we're back to the stopping thing again." She was breathing just as hard.

He smiled and kissed her on the forehead. "Just wait until you get out of here tomorrow."

"I could be out of here tonight, except for that damn doctor."

Paine saw a chair on the other side of the bed. "It's just one night, Abby."

"What now?" She moved her hair out of her eyes.

"Tomorrow, the FBI shows up if they're not here already. They'll do an investigation, see who's involved, and we hope they will close the case."

"Do you think the sheriff's involved?"

Paine frowned. "My gut is saying no, but they'll figure it out."

"You're not going to stay?" Abby asked quietly.

Paine took hold of her hand. "No, honey. We'll all probably be questioned by the FBI, and as soon as they say we can leave, I thought I would drive you back to Portland."

Abby smiled. "I'd like that. But what about Ben?"

"He's here for a couple of days. Jake will stay here with him, and then they'll drive your car back."

Abby gasped. "I forgot about my car. It's not running, Paine."

"It's okay. It's already been towed to a mechanic. He said it would just take a couple of days to fix."

"It looks like you've thought of everything." Abby yawned.

Paine could see that she was getting tired. "Close your eyes, honey. Get some rest."

"They gave me a pain pill, and I feel like I'm floating," she said drowsily.

Paine smiled. "That's good."

"You should go back to the motel."

"Nah, I'm good here."

She smiled. "I think I love you," she whispered right before she fell asleep.

Paine's pulsed raced. *Did she just say she loves me?* He started smiling until a huge grin appeared on his face. *She loves me.*

Jake walked in, saw Paine, and then looked at Abby. He could see that she was sound asleep. "What's so funny?"

Paine turned to him, still smiling. "She loves me."

Jake grinned back at him. "Yep, I figured as much." Then he sighed. "I guess that means I don't have a chance."

Paine laughed. "As I said, don't even try."

Jake walked to the bed and looked at Abby.

"How's Ben?" Paine asked.

"He's a bit of a baby, but he'll be fine."

Paine covered his mouth with his hand and yawned.

"You should go back to the motel and get some rest," Jake said.

Paine shook his head. "No, I want to be here in case she wakes up."

"She'll need you tomorrow, Paine. It's going to be a busy day for her when the FBI gets here." Jake crossed his arms. "I'll stay and take turns watching her and Ben."

Paine hesitated. He was dead on his feet, but the last time he had left her, he had almost lost her.

"I'll keep an eye on her," Jake said as if reading his mind.

Paine still wavered. He knew he couldn't be with her twenty-four-seven for the rest of her life. He stood up, kissed her on the forehead, and brushed a piece of hair away. He looked at Jake. "You watch her. I'll be here first thing in the morning before she wakes up."

Jake nodded. "You got it, Paine."

Paine gave Abby one last look and left the room, telling himself that she was going to be fine.

* * *

Abby slowly woke up. She opened her eyes trying to focus, but everything was fuzzy and distorted. *Where am I?* It was dark, and she couldn't see. She had a moment of panic before she remembered she was in the hospital. Then it all came back to her. Ben and she had been running in the trees, trying to get away from the deputy, and then Paine rescued them. She smiled. Everything was fine now. Tomorrow she would get to go home, and Paine would be with her.

Abby saw a figure sitting in the chair. She closed her eyes again, just too tired to keep them open. She smiled when she felt Paine take her hand, and then she drifted back to sleep.

*　*　*

The next day was busy. Paine was still there when Abby woke up. He stayed with her until after breakfast, but he told her that the FBI was requesting his presence at the sheriff's office. "I've held them off as long as possible, honey."

"It's okay, Paine. Go." He had kissed her until she felt it down to her toes; then he was gone. Now she was sitting there waiting for the doctor to come in and release her. Abby turned on the TV, hoping it would make the time go by faster waiting for him. She surfed through the channels but couldn't find anything that looked interesting to watch. She flicked off the TV and decided she would go visit Ben.

Abby hopped out of bed and groaned. The doctor told her she would be sore, but damn, that hurt. She started for the door and then stopped and looked down at her gown. Then she felt a breeze in the back. She reached behind her and tried closing the gown. She couldn't go visit Ben with her ass hanging out. Then she laughed, thinking it would be ironic now that everything was over that she would still be caught with her ass hanging out.

Still smiling, she walked over to the closet looking for a bathrobe. Abby found one but it was so thin she really didn't think they could call it a bathrobe. Deciding it was just going to have to do, she put it on and headed for Ben's room.

Abby crossed the hall and heard talking in his room. "You don't have to be such a baby," she heard Jake say.

"I'm not being a baby. You're driving me crazy," Ben fired back.

Abby smiled and walked into the room. "Anything I can do in here for you boys?"

Ben smiled in relief when he saw her. "Abby, could you tell this jackass"—he said, looking at Jake—"to go and leave me alone."

Jake turned so Ben wouldn't see and winked at Abby. "That's the thanks I get? I stay here all night watching over you, and I might add, have to listen to you snoring."

Ben started to sputter. "I don't—"

"No, no. It's okay. I'm leaving now," Jake interrupted him. He turned and kissed Abby on the cheek. "Besides, I think Paine might need some moral support with the FBI." And with that he left.

Ben was shaking his head. "Jackass," he muttered under his breath.

"Are you two always like that?" Abby asked.

"It's all in fun, Abby. He's like a brother to me."

Abby sat down in the chair next to the bed. "How are you feeling?"

"Sore, and my ribs hurt like hell, but other than that I'm good. You?"

"Same. I'm sore but I'm ready to get out of here."

"Jake tells me that you and Paine are going to head back to Portland."

Abby sighed. "I hope it's today, but if the doctor doesn't show up soon to release me, it might not happen." She looked down, wiping a piece of lint away. "Then I still have to talk to the FBI."

"You did good out there last night, Abby," Ben said quietly.

Abby smiled at the praise. "So did you. I thought I was going to have a heart attack when I realized you were going to crash the car."

Ben shrugged.

"Thank you for helping me," Abby said quietly. "I was afraid I wouldn't get to see—" Abby stopped.

"You're good for him," Ben said.

She looked at him. "You think so?"

Ben smiled. "I know so." He tried to turn on his side but groaned instead. Abby quickly stood to help him. "Thanks," he said when he was situated. "And besides that, Paine would have had my hide if something had happened to you."

After that they talked about ordinary things. Work, what they did for fun. Ben told her he had a fiancée once, but it hadn't worked out. He told her stories about Jake and his many girlfriends. She was laughing at a story about wine being dumped on Jake when Paine walked in.

"Hey, honey, you ready to get out of here?"

Abby stood and went to him, putting her arm around him. "I am," she said, smiling up at him. Paine bent his head and kissed her. She closed her eyes, wishing they were somewhere else. If he hadn't been holding her, Abby was sure she would have melted into a puddle on the floor. When they broke apart, they just looked at each other.

Ben cleared his throat. "Don't mind me. I'm just stuck here in this bed."

Both Paine and Abby turned to look at him. "Sorry, Ben." She turned pink.

"Don't worry about it, Abby," Ben said, smiling. "If you guys want to get back to Portland today, you better make tracks."

Abby walked over to Ben and kissed him on the cheek. "Thank you again. I'll never forget what you did for me."

This time it was Ben who turned pink. "Get out of here before you make me cry," he said jokingly.

Abby smiled and turned back to Paine. "I'm ready."

"Do what the nurses tell you to do." Paine said to Ben. "Get better, and we'll see you in Portland in a couple of days,"

"Don't worry, boss. I have Jake here to take care of the nurses," Ben joked.

With one last wave to Ben, Paine and Abby walked back to her room. When she walked in and saw her suitcase sitting on the floor next to her bed, Abby jumped in happiness. "My clothes!"

Paine laughed at her excitement. "I figured you were ready for a change of wardrobe."

Abby started to lift the suitcase to the bed, but Paine took it out of her hands and set it down.

She quickly opened it and started rummaging through it, trying to decide what to wear. "It's like getting all new clothes."

After a few minutes of tossing clothes around, she settled on another pair of jeans with a white cashmere sweater. It had been a splurge last year after the school year had ended, but it had been on sale. Abby grabbed some undies and a new bra and headed for the bathroom.

"You can change out here, you know."

Abby laughed. "I don't think so. Remember what happened last time I undressed in front of you?"

He smiled mischievously at her. "Yes, I do." Paine started walking toward her.

Abby was hypnotized by the longing she saw in his eyes. She was pretty sure he saw the same thing in hers. She made a step for him, but just then the nurse walked in.

"I have your discharge papers here for you to sign," she said, unaware she had interrupted anything.

Abby blinked and looked at her. "Um, okay. Can I take a shower first?"

"Sure. I'll come back in fifteen minutes and go through them with you." Then she was gone.

Abby gave Paine a quick peek and then turned and went into the bathroom. She could hear his chuckle as she shut the door.

A half hour later they were on their way to the sheriff's office. Abby was glad to be out of the hospital, but she was not looking forward to having to answer questions for the FBI. "How bad is it?" she asked Paine worriedly.

Paine reached across and squeezed her hand. "It'll be fine, Abby. You'll just go through your story, and then we'll leave."

Abby leaned her head against the seat. "I know. I'm just ready to go home now." She turned to look at him when he started to clear his throat. She frowned anxiously at him. "What's wrong?"

Paine put his hand back on the wheel. "Um, nothing's wrong."

Abby waited for him to continue, and when he didn't, she asked again. "Paine, I can tell something's wrong. So you might as well tell me."

Abby saw Paine take a deep breath, putting her nerves more on edge. "Do you remember anything about last night?"

She frowned. "When last night? At the hospital?"

"Right before you went to sleep."

Abby thought about it and ran everything in her mind of how the night went. She had been checked over by the doctor, and he told her she would have to stay the night. Then being in her room. Paine came in later and helped her with the bed. They were talking. And then it hit her.

No, no, no. Did I say I love you out loud?

Abby was mortified. He probably wanted to tell her it was too soon, or he wanted to break it to her gently that he didn't feel the same way. She couldn't look at him. She turned her head to look out the window.

"Abby?"

"No, I don't really remember much about last night," she lied.

"I think you do," Paine said quietly.

"Paine, just forget it, okay? I was high on pain pills, remember?"

"Abby, look at me."

"No."

"Please."

You might as well get it over with. Abby sighed and turned her head to look at him. "What?" she asked warily.

"I wanted to wait to have this conversation when we had more time, but we're going to be busy for the next several hours, and I can't wait that long."

"I told you, Paine, it's okay. We don't have to have the conservation at all."

"Damn it, Abby, yes, we do."

"Okay, okay. You don't have to snap at me," she growled back.

She waited. Abby started to get annoyed when he didn't say anything. "Well?" she asked impatiently.

Paine looked at her. "You told me last night that you loved me."

Abby groaned in misery. "I'm sorry, Paine. I didn't know I said it out loud."

"Do you? Love me?" he asked quietly.

This is not how Abby pictured this day going. She had had images of her and Paine riding the ferry, walking the decks holding hands, and putting this whole nightmare behind them. "It was the pain-killers talking."

"So you don't love me then?" he asked bitterly.

"I didn't say that, but it's only been a few days and"—she paused—"I'm sorry if it freaked you out." Miserable, she once again looked out the window.

Abby turned to look at him when he started pulling the car over to the side of the road. "What are you doing?"

"I'm stopping."

"I can see that," she said, infuriated. "Why?"

"Because I want to see your face when I tell you that I love you, too!"

Abby gasped, and her heart started thumping in her chest. "You love me?" she squeaked.

Paine didn't say anything until he stopped and had turned off the car. He turned to look at her then. "I'm not going to lie to you, Abby, but it scares the hell out of me."

Abby didn't know how to respond, so she just waited.

"After my divorce, I thought it would be years before I would be ready to put my heart at risk again."

Abby swallowed.

"But then you showed up at my door, and all hell broke loose. Then last night, when I almost lost you?" He ran his hand through his hair again.

Abby hid her smile.

"What I'm trying to say is that I love you, and I hope you feel the same." He was almost pleading.

Abby's heart pounded in her chest. *He loves me.* She scooted over the seat and put her hand around his neck and kissed him. She moved, trying to get on his lap, but the steering wheel was in the way. Still kissing her, he moved them both so they were sitting in the middle and Abby was able to straddle his lap. She could feel his erection against her. Abby started to rock against him and heard him groan.

"Abby you're killing me," he whispered before he captured her mouth again.

Abby quickly unbuttoned his shirt and ran her hands over his chest. He took her sweater and lifted it over her head. Then he pushed her down so she was lying on the seat with him on top.

"We can't do this here, honey," Paine said between kisses.

"Yes, we can," she said breathlessly. "I don't want you to stop, Paine."

She forgot about everything else except Paine telling her he loved her.

17

Paine watched Abby from across the room. The FBI had been questioning her for hours now. She seemed to be holding up okay, but he was starting to see dark circles under her eyes.

After they had made love in the car, which Paine still couldn't believe, they had arrived later than he had wanted to. When they had walked in, Paine had apologized for being late, and he had seen Abby turn pink. She probably wouldn't make a very good poker player. Jake had been sitting at a desk, talking on the phone, and had given Paine a knowing smile and a wink. Paine had smiled back and shrugged. He loved Abby and didn't care who knew it.

Paine heard the agent ask another question. "So you knew the deputy was involved when he said his name was Hank?"

Abby sighed. "Agent Miller, I don't know how many times I have to say it." Paine could hear the fatigue in her voice and decided it was enough.

"Ms. Turner, we're just trying to make sure we have it all straight and what your role was in it."

"What are you saying, Agent Miller?" Abby asked furiously.

Paine stepped behind her and put his hand on her shoulder. "I think we're done here." He scowled at the agent. He was a typical FBI agent, dressed in a dark suit. His hair was cut short, and he had dark-rimmed glasses perched on the end of his nose.

The agent stood up and faced Paine. "No, we're not done."

"We're done," he said firmly, reaching down to help Abby out of her chair. "If you have any more questions, you can ask her in Portland. But now, we're leaving."

Paine started for the door, with Jake following behind them.

"We'll be in touch, Ms. Turner," the agent said.

They left the building and headed for the car. "He makes it sound like I'm guilty of something," Abby said, still angry.

"Don't worry about it, Abby," Jake said, leaning against Paine's car. "They all act like that because their ties are too tight."

Abby laughed. "Thanks, Jake."

Jake turned to Paine. "Are you still heading out tonight?"

Paine looked at his watch and realized they'd probably already missed the last ferry. He hadn't checked out of their rooms, just in case. "No, we'll stay at the motel tonight and leave first thing in the morning."

Jake nodded. "I talked with Ben earlier, and they might let him out tomorrow. If they do, we'll go sometime tomorrow if Abby's car is ready."

"I appreciate you guys driving my car back," Abby said, looking to Paine. "I can drive it back myself if that would be better for you."

Before Jake could answer, Paine spoke. "No, Abby. They can drive your car, and you'll ride with me."

"It's my car, Paine. I think I can decide if I should drive it back or not."

Paine could tell she was getting angry and tried to tone it down a bit. "I know you can, honey. I just want you with me." Because there was no way in hell she was going to drive back by herself.

"Oh," she said, the fight going out of her. "Well then, I guess you and Ben can drive my car back." She smiled at Jake.

Jake grinned back. "It will be our pleasure."

"You might not say that after driving it," Abby said. "It can be a bit temperamental."

Jake snorted. "I'm used to dealing with temperamental things," he said, looking toward Paine.

Paine scowled at him but didn't say anything. Instead he turned to Abby. "You ready to go?" He reached around Jake to open the passenger-side door.

Jake stepped aside to make room for Abby. "I'm heading over to the hospital to check on Ben, and then I'll probably go to the motel." He looked pointedly at Paine.

"We get it, Jake. We'll make sure the adjoining door is closed," Abby said before climbing into the car.

After his shock wore off, Paine laughed. "Yeah, so don't knock unless you're about to be killed or something."

"Wouldn't think of it, boss." Jake grinned.

*   *   *

They were lying in bed holding each other after having made love for the second time. Paine decided he was starting to like the whole shower thing. The first time had been in the bed, but then Abby had wanted to shower, so he had joined her. Now they had the TV on, but neither of them were really watching it. Paine kissed her on top of her head. "How are you feeling?"

Abby yawned and stretched. "Mm, pretty good," she purred.

Paine laughed. "I'm talking about if you're sore or not."

"Oh." She smiled. "It's better than it was this morning."

"They say the second day is always worse."

Abby yawned again. "I'm sure it will be fine."

"We could always just stay in bed tomorrow if you want," Paine whispered in her ear.

Abby turned so her butt and back were against Paine's chest. He put his arm over her waist. "It's tempting, but I need to get back."

Paine started kissing her ear. "You smell good."

"So do you," she said faintly. "It's nice with you holding me. Oh, and thanks for holding my hand last night when I woke up."

Paine frowned and lifted his head to look at her. "When, Abby?" She didn't answer because she was already asleep. He laid his head next to her and told himself to ask her in the morning. Then he fell asleep.

* * *

The next day they left early. It had taken Abby longer than usual to get ready. Paine was right. It was worse the second day. All of her muscles were protesting at once. It was even worse than the time she let her friend talk her into walking a twenty-mile marathon for charity.

She was trying to comb her hair when Paine walked into the bathroom. "You okay, honey?"

"Just peachy," she grumbled. He laughed and took the comb from her and proceeded to comb her hair for her. Abby decided it was the sexiest thing a man had ever done for her.

They reached Seattle by noon and decided to stop for lunch. They chose a diner that was right off an exit so they wouldn't have to fight traffic. They were sitting in a booth across from each other.

"Good choice," Abby said, munching on her hamburger. She had been starving and was about ready to eat her napkin when the waitress had brought their lunch.

Paine was smiling at her.

"What?" she asked self-consciously.

"Nothing, honey. I just like it that you enjoy food."

Abby snorted. "Who doesn't?" She took another big bite.

Twenty minutes later, Abby was moaning and feeling miserable. "Why did you let me eat so much?"

Paine laughed. "I didn't let you do anything. Honey, that was all you."

Abby groaned again. "I don't ever want to eat again."

"That's too bad. I was hoping to take you to dinner tonight."

"Really? Like a date?"

Paine laughed. "Yeah, like a date."

"I'd like that," Abby said with a big smile.

Four hours later, they pulled into Abby's driveway. She was exhausted and stiff from being in the car for so long. They had made a couple of pit stops, but other than that, they had driven straight through.

She watched as Paine got out of the car and headed for the passenger door. Once he had it opened, she moved to get out. "Ow, Paine. It hurts so bad."

"I know, honey. I'm sorry." He reached down for her hand. "Come on now. Very slowly." Abby felt like she had been used as a punching bag. After five minutes of torture, she was finally out of the car. Then she looked up and groaned inside. Her front door seemed a long way away.

"I could carry you," Paine said, looking at her.

Damn, does he always know what I'm thinking?

"No, I can do it." Abby started for her door.

"I'm going to grab your suitcase."

"Okay," Abby said absently, trying to talk herself into taking the first step. *Come on, Abby, you can't stand out here all day*. The first step was the worst, and she decided the second wasn't any better, but somehow she made it to the front door. Paine had gotten her keys out of her purse and opened the door.

They both turned when they heard someone calling her name.

Abby cringed but turned and smiled. "Hi, Ashley."

Abby watched Ashley spring up her stairs. *That must be nice,* she thought.

"Hey, you're back." Ashley gave Abby a quick hug. She wanted to cry out in pain but held it back. She was just happy that Ashley didn't seem to be upset with her anymore.

Then Ashley turned to look at Paine.

"Paine, this is my neighbor, Ashley."

Paine stuck his hand out for her to shake. "It's nice to meet you, Ashley."

Ashley hesitated for a second before shaking his hand. "It's nice to meet you, too," she said. She turned back to Abby. "You're back early."

"Yeah, well, you won't believe what happened on my vacation."

"I can't wait to hear it," Ashley said with enthusiasm.

Abby cringed. She just wanted to crawl in her bed and sleep until next year. After she took some aspirin first. She gave Paine a desperate look.

"I think Abby will have to tell you that story later, Ashley," Paine said, opening the door.

"I'm sorry, and who are you again?" Ashley asked sharply.

Abby looked at her in surprise. "Ashley, Paine is my…" She hesitated. *What is Paine exactly?* "Paine is…"

"I'm Abby's boyfriend."

It was Ashley's turn to look surprised. "Well, that didn't take long," she said unkindly.

Abby could feel the heat on her face. "What do you mean, Ashley?" she asked defensively.

"Oh nothing, Abby." She smiled. "I didn't mean anything by it."

Abby didn't believe her but let it go. "I'm sorry, Ashley, but I really need to go in now." She was exhausted and didn't want to fight with her anymore.

"Um, sure, Abby." Ashley started down the stairs. "I'll come by later." She waved.

"What's her problem?" Paine asked, watching her walk away.

"I don't know. She and Jeff seem be going through something, and right now I really don't care."

"Jeff?" Paine asked.

"Ashley's husband." Paine opened the door, and she headed straight for her bedroom. "I have to take some aspirin," Abby said over her shoulder.

"Why don't you take a pain pill?"

Abby stopped. *That's right. I have pain pills.* She turned and headed back for her purse.

"I like your house," Paine said.

"Thanks." She was still trying to find the pills. "It's over seventy years old, but I recently had it renovated." Abby turned her purse a different way to find the pills. *Where were the damn pills?*

"Here, give it to me," Paine said, taking the purse from her.

Handing it over, Abby sat down on the couch. She looked around. She had missed her home. Her living room and kitchen were open. A hallway led to a spare bedroom, an extra bathroom, and then her room. She had gotten the house cheap, so she had the extra money to renovate. She had chosen natural colors for walls and counter tops but had accented with bright cheery colors. Her couch was a deep purple with white pillows that were sprinkled with the same color of purple. Two white armchairs sat across from it with bright orange pillows.

"Here you go, honey." Paine held out two small pills.

Abby opened her hand, and he dropped them into it. "I'll get you some water."

She tried to lean back against the couch, but it was just too painful, so she was sitting the same way when Paine came back with the water.

Abby took the pills and prayed they worked quickly. "I think I'm going to have to take a rain check for dinner, Paine."

He sat down next to her. "It's okay. We'll have many other opportunities to have dinner."

She smiled shyly at him. "I hope so."

"I'm with you, Abby. It's where I want to be."

Abby tried to raise her arms to hug him but ended up groaning instead. "This sucks," she grumbled.

Paine laughed. "Why don't you lie down for a while and let the pain pills kick in? I'll go to the office and check in, and I'll come back later."

"That would be nice." She got up very slowly and turned to him. "I'm afraid I'm going to have to ask for a favor."

"Anything, honey."

"Can you help me get undressed?"

"I'd thought you would never ask."

She looked up at him. "I mean, I won't be able to do it by myself."

Paine smiled and tweaked her nose. "I know, honey." He took her hand and led her down the hallway to her bedroom. Her room was her favorite of the whole house. It was large, even with a king-size bed and dresser in it. The bed was covered with a bright-blue comforter accented with lime-green pillows. It had a large walk-in closet with an en suite bathroom. She had gutted the bathroom to make room for her claw foot bathtub. Abby loved soaking in it after a long day at school.

It took twenty minutes to get undressed with Paine's help. Abby thought she would be embarrassed, but Paine had been a gentleman and was all business. He helped her put on some yoga pants with an oversize T-shirt. Now her eyes were getting heavy, and all she wanted to do was lie on her bed and sleep.

Abby walked out of her bathroom after brushing her teeth and saw Paine standing by her bed with the covers folded back. "Hop in, honey."

Abby smiled and slipped into the covers.

"Scoot over, Abby."

She turned to look at Paine in surprise.

"I'm just going to stay until you're asleep."

She smiled and moved over, thanking the heavens for whoever invented pain pills.

Abby didn't know that forty-five minutes later, Paine slipped out of the bed and went to his car, or that he hadn't noticed a man sitting in a car parked down the street.

18

Jake walked into Ben's hospital room and was glad to see he was dressed and ready to go. "You ready to blow this joint?" he asked.

"Yeah, I'm ready," Ben said, holding his ribs. They still hurt like hell.

"Abby's car wasn't ready yet, but it should be by the time we get over there. The mechanic said he would stay open until we got there," Jake said. "I talked to Paine earlier, and they're back in Portland, and he said Abby was really sore."

"I feel her pain." Ben winced as he tried to put on his shoes.

Jake walked over to help Ben and took his shoe out of his hand.

"What are you doing?" Ben asked.

"I'm going help you put on your shoes."

"No, you're not." Ben took the shoe back.

"Yes, I am." Jake once again took the shoe out of Ben's hand.

"I said I could do it, jackass." Ben glared at Jake and ripped the shoe out of his hand.

"And I say you're being a baby again." Jake reached for the shoe, but Ben held it away from him.

"Do you want me to hit you with this thing?" Ben asked, shaking the shoe at Jake.

"Is there a problem in here?"

They both turned and looked at the nurse, who was pushing a wheelchair.

Jake stood and smiled at the nurse. "No, ma'am. My friend here is just being a baby."

"I am not a baby," Ben growled.

Jake kept smiling at the nurse. "See?"

The nurse shook her head and started helping Ben put on his shoes. Jake watched. "I was just trying to do the same thing," he said to the nurse.

"Just be quiet, Jake," Ben mumbled. He hated the feeling of being helpless, but it was less embarrassing to have the nurse do it.

Jake just shrugged and waited while the nurse finished.

Twenty minutes later they were riding in a taxi on their way to the mechanic's. "By the way, you owe me two hundred dollars." Jake grinned at Ben.

Ben laughed and then winced in pain. "Damn, that hurts."

"Take a pain pill," Jake suggested.

"I did," Ben said. "Right before we left the hospital. Just waiting for it to kick in."

"You still owe me two hundred bucks."

"I know, Jake," Ben said, smiling. "It's fun to watch Paine being bossed around for once."

Jake laughed. "I think he's met his match. She's almost as bossy as he is."

They both were laughing when the taxi pulled into the auto shop parking lot. Jake paid the driver and was the first one out. Ben moved slowly behind him. They walked into the garage, and Jake could see Abby's car parked in a corner.

"Hey, buddy," Jake said, kicking the foot of a man who was lying under a car.

The man rolled out. "How you doing?" He stood up and started wiping his hands on a dirty cloth.

"We're here to pick up that car over there." Jake pointed to Abby's car.

"Yes, sir. It's ready to go," the man said, heading for an office in the garage. "The cut radiator hose, right?"

Jake and Ben looked at each other, frowning. "What do you mean, cut?" Ben asked.

"There was a small cut in the hose"—the mechanic frowned—"which is strange, because it looked like a brand-new hose."

"Did it look like it was deliberately cut?" Jake asked anxiously. He was starting to get a bad feeling.

The man shrugged. "I can't say for sure, but it's a very straight cut. So yes, I would guess it was cut with a knife."

Ben and Jake looked at each other. "Abby's car broke down *before* she saw the man murdered," Jake said, thinking out loud.

"Yeah, so that means somebody would have had to cut it before that." Ben turned to the mechanic. "How long would a car run with a bad radiator hose before it broke down?"

"Oh, I don't know. It could vary."

"Well, take your best guess," Ben said impatiently.

"Half hour to forty-five minutes."

"Abby would have been on the ferry then. Right?" Ben asked, looking at Jake.

Jake shook his head. "That would mean somebody on the ferry cut the hose."

"But why?" Ben asked, frowning. "Who would do that?"

"Maybe our second shooter wasn't the deputy after all," Jake said, pacing. "That would mean somebody else is after Abby."

"We need to call Paine." Ben reached for his phone.

*   *   *

The Black Angel watched the man move toward the woman's house. He watched him climb up her stairs to the front door. Finding it locked, he turned and looked around. The Black Angel knew the man couldn't see him. He was well hidden, and besides, this guy was such an idiot, he wouldn't notice a grenade if it went off in front of him.

The Black Angel watched him run down the stairs and head for the back of the house. He followed him just to make sure he didn't do something stupid like getting caught. He had his own plans for the man *and* the woman. Now the man was at the back door and seemed to be trying to pick the lock. The Black Angel was surprised when the door opened and the man disappeared inside. He smiled and left.

*   *   *

She opened her eyes very slowly, her heart pounding in her chest. She could feel somebody in the room. She could hear him breathing, and his clothes were making little swishy noises when he moved. Her ringing phone had woken her up, but she had known immediately that someone else was there.

Abby closed her eyes again and tried to keep her breathing normal. She didn't want to let whoever this was know she was awake. Maybe he would take whatever he wanted and leave her alone.

She had woken an hour ago and looked for Paine, but he was gone. Abby had quickly fallen back to sleep. Now there was somebody in her room, and she knew it wasn't Paine. *Who is this? What does he want? I just got out of one nightmare, and now I'm living another one.*

She could hear him move by her bed, and she was sure he had stopped where her head was. She kept still. *He must be standing there just looking at me.* She was sure he could hear her pounding heart. Abby had to hold back a scream when she felt somebody very softly touch her hand. It made her think back to that night in the hospital. She thought it had been Paine, but now she wasn't sure.

The man kept rubbing her hand almost like a caress. *Paine, where are you?* she cried in her head.

"I know you're awake, Abby," the man said softly.

Abby opened her eyes. It was so dark that she didn't see anything at first. Then a shadow moved in front of her. Abby let out a cry and quickly moved to the other side of the bed.

"It's okay, Abby. I'm here now," the man whispered.

Abby thought the voice was familiar, but with him whispering, she couldn't be sure.

"What do you want?" Abby asked, her heart in her throat.

The shadow sat down on the bed. Abby's eyes had adjusted to the dark, and she could see the shape of a large man dressed in black. She still couldn't see his face clearly, though.

"I just wanted us to be together, Abby. I knew you wanted that, too, but you were just being shy," the man said, still whispering.

"I don't even know who you are." Abby stood up from the bed and looked at her bedroom door. "What do you want?" *I could make it. I could be out the door before the man even moved,* Abby thought.

The man ran at her. Abby ran for the door, but he grabbed her from behind before she could get to it. He slung her away from it, and she landed on the floor. Abby got up and ran for her bathroom. She was almost to the door when he tackled her from behind again. This time she landed hard on the floor, hitting her cheek. She tried to ignore the pain and started thrashing, trying to get loose. Abby could hear the man breathing hard.

"Stop fighting me, Abby."

Abby stopped moving and turned to look at her attacker. *No, it can't be!* "Jeff?"

"I just wanted us to be together, but you had to go and ruin everything," Jeff whined.

"I don't know what you're talking about, Jeff. You're married to Ashley."

Jeff snorted. "That bitch is nothing but a"—Jeff laughed—"well, a bitch."

Abby struggled, but Jeff pulled her inch by inch back to him. *I need to stall him. Paine will come. Paine will come.* Abby kept repeating it in her head.

"Jeff, I'm sorry if I did something to make you think I was interested in—"

"Stop it!" Jeff screamed, pulling out a knife. Abby froze. "You wanted me until Ashley interfered. I know she told you to stay away, and that's why you planned your vacation."

"You're right, Jeff," Abby said quietly. "Let's talk about it and see if we can work it out."

Abby tried to think of what to do. If she started kicking, she was afraid he would cut her. *What choice do I have, though?* It was a risk she was going to have to take.

By twisting and thrashing, Abby got one foot loose. She kicked him in the face, and she heard a crack. Jeff roared in pain and let her go. She quickly got up and ran the rest of the way into the bathroom. She slammed the door and locked it. Leaning against it, Abby was breathing hard, trying to think. *Where is my phone?* Her heart sank; it was in her purse in the living room. She turned on the bathroom light and blinked. *I need a weapon,* she thought, looking around.

The door suddenly shook behind her, and she jumped away from it. "There is nowhere for you to go, Abby," Jeff said, shaking the door handle. "I'm sorry. I didn't mean to scare you."

"Just go away, Jeff, and I won't say anything to Ashley," she pleaded.

The door shook again and again. Jeff was trying to break it down. Abby started opening drawers, looking for anything she could use as a weapon.

Where are you, Paine?

*   *   *

Paine was sitting at his desk when Bill walked in. He was another detective whom Paine trusted with his life. Bill had also been part of the team along with Jake and Ben who had helped with the stalking case. He was the oldest of them all, and he was also the most soft-spoken, which Paine thought was strange, considering he was such a big man.

Bill took a seat in front of Paine's desk. "I hear you had some trouble."

Paine leaned back in his chair, smiling. "Yeah, just a little."

"Jake told me there was a cop involved," he said in disgust.

Paine nodded. The stalking case also involved a cop. Paine hoped this was the last of dealing with dirty cops. "I don't know everything yet, but the FBI is still working it all out. It looks like drugs were being smuggled in with help from a few deputies and some border patrols."

"Sounds like quite an operation."

Paine leaned forward, putting his elbows on his desk. "So far, they can't find a connection with the sheriff, but they're still digging. It will probably be months before it's all worked out."

"So who's Abby?" Bill asked softly.

Paine couldn't help smiling. "Have you been gossiping with Ben and Jake?"

"No. I just know there was a girl involved. And—"

Paine held up his hand to stop Bill. "It's okay, Bill. I was just teasing."

That made Bill frown.

"What?" Paine asked.

Bill smiled. "Just never saw you tease before. She must be quite a girl."

Paine shrugged. "What can I say, Bill? I love her." Paine saw Bill's surprised look. He couldn't blame him. It still surprised him how quickly he fell for Abby. Paine had never believed in love at first sight, but now he wasn't so sure. He just knew he wanted no one else except Abby, and he couldn't wait to get back to her.

"Well, when do I get to meet her?"

Paine started to respond when his phone rang. "Ben? Are you guys back already?"

"Paine, are you with Abby?" Ben asked quickly.

"Ben, what's wrong?"

Ben paused. "It may be nothing."

"What may be nothing?" Paine snapped.

"Jake and I are here picking up Abby's car."

Paine could hear Ben taking a breath. "Damn it, Ben. What is it?"

"The mechanic thinks her radiator hose was *deliberately* cut."

Paine felt the blood drain from his face. He was sure his heart had stopped beating. "What are you saying?" he choked out.

"It was cut *before* the murder!"

Paine ran a hand through his hair. "How do you know that?" He didn't want it to be true but knew in his heart it was. He had always felt something wasn't right about the whole thing.

"Paine, somebody meant for her to break down on that road," Ben said anxiously.

Paine hung up the phone and immediately called Abby's phone. It just rang and rang. *Please, honey, pick up.*

"What's wrong, Paine?" Bill looked concerned.

Paine ignored him and dialed her number again. Abby still didn't pick up. He started out of his office door. Bill grabbed his arm. "Paine, what's wrong?"

Paine jerked his arm free. "Abby's in trouble." He started running to his car with Bill behind him.

In the car, Paine got on his radio and asked for any unit closest to Abby's house to respond. Then he threw his phone at Bill. "Keep calling her."

Bill took the phone and dialed while looking at Paine. "She could be fine, Paine."

"Shut up, Bill," Paine shouted. "She's in trouble. I knew something wasn't right."

"How?" Bill shouted back. "How could you know?" Any other time Paine would have been surprised by Bill's outburst, but now all he could think about was Abby.

"Because he was always there. He always knew where we were." Paine struck the steering wheel. "How could I have been so stupid?"

"You need to calm down, Paine."

"Screw you, Bill."

"Paine, I'm telling you as a friend and a cop that you need to think about Abby right now and stop feeling sorry for yourself," Bill said, back to his calm self. "She needs you, the cop, not some out-of-control lover."

Paine wanted to kick and scream, but in his heart he knew Bill was right. He needed to start acting like a cop and start thinking about what they were going to face when they got to Abby's. Paine was calmer now, but it didn't stop him from saying a silent prayer. *Please, God, let her be okay.*

19

The door flew open, and Jeff stood there, smiling at her. She'd always thought Jeff looked like a chipmunk. His hair was reddish brown with a streak of blond running down one side, and his cheeks were full like he was storing food for the winter. At one time she thought he had kind eyes, but right now they were full of rage. He looked like a crazy man with blood dripping down his nose.

"You bitch." He wiped his hand under his nose and flicked the blood at Abby. It landed on her face and neck. He moved toward her.

"You probably shouldn't have done that," Abby said, trying not to gag.

"Done what?"

Wait, Abby. When he stood in front of her, he grabbed her arm. "Done what, Abby?" he asked menacingly.

"I don't do blood." She managed to say before throwing up on him.

He jumped back in disgust, looking down at his clothes. It was all the distraction Abby needed. She lifted up the scissors she had found in the drawer and stabbed him in the shoulder. He looked up at her with surprise. Then his eyes turned angry, and he tried to reach for her again, but she jumped out of the way and went around him. He grabbed her T-shirt, but Abby quickly turned back to him and pushed on the scissors in his shoulder, trying not to throw up again.

He screamed and fell to his knees. Abby turned and ran out of the bathroom and then shrieked when she saw a figure standing in front of her bedroom door. She stopped and just looked at him.

Now who's this?

Abby couldn't help but think this was the most bizarre week of her life. *This* man was dressed in all black, and his face was covered in some kind of black makeup, but it was the gun he was holding that had her frozen in place. He took a step forward. Abby backed up, knowing Jeff was behind her, but she figured right now he was the lesser of two evils.

"I'm not here for you, Abby," he said quietly.

"Do I know you?" Abby asked nervously.

"Not really, but I was with you in the woods."

Abby frowned in confusion. "I don't understand. What do you mean you were in the woods?" She thought about it, and then she knew. "You were the one trying to kill me?"

"At first."

Abby had no idea who this man was or what he wanted; she just wanted out of this room. She turned back to look at Jeff. He was still on his knees, but he wasn't looking at her. He was looking at the stranger in the doorway, and he looked terrified.

He's here for Jeff.

Abby turned back to the man. "You want Jeff?"

The man nodded.

"But why?"

The man took a step closer. Abby's instinct was to step back, but she stayed where she was. "Why do you want Jeff?"

"Because he lied, and I can't have that." The man took another step. "You can go, Abby. You won't ever see me again. I give you my word."

Abby wanted to run out of the room, but instead she looked back at Jeff. He was still on his knees with blood dripping from his nose. The scissors weren't in his shoulder anymore, but his shirt was soaked with blood. He was looking between her and the man, pleading with his eyes for her help.

Can I just leave him here, helpless? He just tried to kill you, Abby. Doesn't he deserve it?

Abby didn't know if he deserved it or not, but she knew she couldn't leave him here with this man.

"Can you tell me why you want to kill Jeff?" she asked him more boldly than she felt.

The man looked at her and chuckled. "I knew I had it wrong when I watched you helping that cop out of the wrecked car."

"You were there?" Abby whispered.

"I told you, Abby. I've been with you since your car died on that road."

Abby was trying to work through this in her head. "You were trying to kill me, right?"

"That's right."

"Then why didn't you?" Abby couldn't believe she was standing here talking calmly to a man who tried to kill her several times in the last few days. Then another thought occurred to her. "How did you know where we were all the time?"

"I tracked you, but the cop kept getting in the way. Then the bald man tried to kill you in that diner, so I had to take care of him." The man smiled. "He deserved it, and besides, I was having too much fun for him to spoil it." He turned and looked at Jeff, and his smile vanished. "Then I realized I had been lied to."

Abby looked at Jeff. "I still don't understand. What does Jeff have to do with all this?"

The man looked at Abby again. "He told me you were trying to kill his wife so that you two could be together."

Abby looked at Jeff, stunned. "Why would you say that?"

"I love you, Abby," Jeff said, spitting out blood. "I tried to show you at our party last month."

Abby thought back to that night. Ashley and Jeff were having a Halloween party, and she went dressed as Tinker Bell because she was reading the book in her class. She hadn't wanted to go but had felt obligated. She had been feeling uncomfortable around Ashley and Jeff and wasn't sure what was wrong, but she had gone and actually had a good time. She didn't remember anything unusual happening, though. "I don't know what you mean, Jeff."

"I gave you a book of poems. I told you to read every single one, because some things are better said on paper." He sounded pitiful.

Abby remembered the book, but she didn't remember him saying anything like that. She shook her head. "I'm sorry, Jeff. I just thought it was a book you wanted me to read."

He laughed humorlessly. "I knew you didn't understand," he said and wiped the blood again from his nose. Abby tried to avoid looking. "I knew you would never be mine."

Abby jumped when the stranger spoke next to her. She hadn't realized that he had moved. "And I'm assuming that's when he decided to hire me."

"You hired someone to kill me?" she asked, shocked.

"It was a mistake," he said, trying to stand. "Please, Abby. Try to understand. I love you, and I know I made a mistake." Jeff was standing now, leaning against the doorframe.

"I *don't* understand, Jeff," Abby said, disgusted. "You hired someone to kill me!"

She saw the man moving toward Jeff. "Go now, Abby," he said menacingly. "I'll take care of this."

Jeff started pleading. "I said I was sorry. You don't have to do this."

Abby almost felt sorry for him. *He tried to kill you, Abby. What's there to feel sorry for?*

"Please, Abby!" Jeff begged.

Abby knew she would never forgive herself if she let Jeff die. No matter how she felt about him, she couldn't let someone die if she could stop it. She reached for the man's arm to stop him. "You don't have to kill him. It's over now, and the police can take care of him."

"Don't mistake me for a nice guy, Abby." He looked down at her hand holding his arm. She quickly dropped her hand, her heart in her throat. "It's not your decision." He started moving toward Jeff.

Jeff started screaming. "No, no, no." He moved away from the doorframe and started moving back into the bathroom.

Abby jumped in front of the stranger. "Please! You can just walk away. The police will arrest him, and he'll go to prison." She turned and looked at Jeff cowered in a corner. "Look at him. How well do you think he would do in jail?"

The man pushed Abby aside and brought up his gun.

"Please!" she begged again. Abby watched in horror as the man took aim and fired at Jeff. Abby let out a scream and turned to look at Jeff. He had fallen to the floor and was holding his leg, screaming in pain. He wasn't dead. She turned and looked at the man in surprise.

"She just saved you," the man said in disgust to Jeff.

Abby rushed over to Jeff to help him. She grabbed a towel off the rack and knelt down to put it over his wound. She started to gag and had to turn her head. That's when she noticed the man was gone.

Abby stood and went back into her room and looked around. There was no trace of him ever being there. He had simply disappeared.

"Abby, help me!"

With one last look around, she went back to Jeff. He was still holding his leg, tears coming down his cheeks. "He shot me. The bastard shot me."

"Shut up, Jeff, or I swear...I'll shoot you, too."

Jeff didn't say anything else, and Abby heard sirens outside her house.

* * *

Paine and Bill slowly stepped through the front door of Abby's house. Really all he wanted to do was rush in and find her. He was holding his gun in front of him, calling her name in his head. *Where is she?* He motioned for Bill to check the kitchen, and he started moving toward her bedroom. He could hear voices coming from the back of the room. He let out a breath when he heard Abby's voice. "I'm going to puke all over you again if you don't stop bellyaching."

Paine smiled. *She's safe. Thank you, God.* He went into her bedroom and saw her sitting on the floor with some man who seemed to be crying. Paine looked around just to make sure there was no one else in the room. When he decided the room was clear, he headed for the bathroom. "Abby."

Abby looked up at him, stood, and jumped into his arms. "You're here."

Paine held her tight. "I'm here, honey." He didn't think he could ever let her go. She was safe and in his arms. Paine didn't know how long they stood there holding each other before Bill came up behind him.

"I called for an ambulance."

Abby was pulling away from him. He didn't want to let her go. He knew he was going to have to sooner or later, but he kept holding her hand. Paine turned to Bill. "Has the cavalry arrived?"

"They're here, and we need to let them in this room."

Paine turned back to Abby and really saw her face for the first time. His heart jumped into his throat when he saw she was covered in blood. "Abby, are you hurt?"

She dismissed his concern. "I'm fine, Paine." She turned and looked down at the man on the floor. "Jeff needs a doctor, though."

Paine looked at the man on the floor. "Jeff, your neighbor?"

"Yep, that would be the one," Abby said with disgust.

Paine frowned. "What does he have to do with all this?"

Abby started to explain when the paramedics came through the door. Bill, Paine, and she moved out of the way so they could get to Jeff. They all watched while they worked on him. Jeff complained the whole time. Paine wanted to put a sock in his mouth to shut him up, and he had so many questions, it was hard for him to be patient and wait.

After twenty minutes, they were finally ready to move Jeff out. Abby turned and walked out into her living room with Paine following. She hadn't said anything for a while, and Paine was starting to get worried. The stretcher holding Jeff started to pass Abby when he grabbed her arm. Paine made a move for the man, but Abby stopped him.

"It's okay, Paine."

Paine didn't like it, but he held back.

"I love you, Abby," the man said miserably. "You have to understand. I did it because I love you."

"That's not love, Jeff." Abby freed her arm from his grasp. "That's just insanity."

The paramedics moved the stretcher out the door, and he was gone. Paine waited. He wasn't sure what to do for Abby. She seemed to be lost in her thoughts. After a few minutes, she turned to him and smiled. He opened his arms, and she walked into them and held him tight.

"Are you okay?" he asked.

"I'm sad and disappointed and relieved all at the same time," she whispered.

Paine pulled away. "Let's sit down."

"I need to wash my face," Abby said, wiping some blood off her face.

"You sit. I'll go get a wet cloth." Paine went to the kitchen and grabbed a towel, ran it under the faucet, and went back to Abby. She was still sitting on the couch looking at nothing. He sat down next to her and started wiping the blood from her face.

She stopped him. "I can do it, Paine."

He gave her the cloth and waited while she finished. "Can you tell me what happened tonight?"

Abby gave him a lopsided smile. "I'm not sure if I totally understand it myself, but I'll give it a try."

A half hour later, Paine couldn't believe what Abby told him. "So let me get this straight. You had the bald man after you because you saw him murder a man, and then you had a killer for hire after you because your neighbor loves you and wanted you dead." Paine took a breath. "And the hired killer wanted to kill Jeff because he lied?" He was incredulous.

"That about sums it up," Abby said dejectedly. "I still can't believe it was Jeff. I thought he was my friend."

Paine hated seeing her looking miserable. "Honey, there are all kinds of sick people out there. You just happened to be a neighbor to one."

Abby looked at him and gave him a small smile. "Lucky me."

Paine chuckled and kissed her softly on the mouth. He pulled away and put his forehead against hers. "I love you, Abby. I thought I was going to be too late, and I'm not sure what I would have done."

"Everything's fine now, Paine. You're here, and the hired killer is gone."

Paine lifted his head. "How do we know he won't come back? What if you're still in danger?" Paine stood, not able to keep still.

Abby stood too and reached for him. "He won't come back. He gave me his word."

Paine snorted. "Well, then. Since a hired killer gave you his word, it must be okay," he said sarcastically and started to pace again. "I knew something wasn't right."

"Paine, you're making me nervous."

Paine stopped in front of her. "I'm sorry, honey. Did the man say anything else to give us a clue to who he is?"

Abby shook her head. "He just said that he tracked me and that you kept getting in the way."

Paine frowned, shaking his head. "How did he track you?" It still didn't totally make sense to him.

Abby shrugged. "He didn't say, and I didn't ask." She sat back down on the couch. "I'm tired, Paine, and I just don't want to think about it anymore right now."

Paine sat down next to her. "You're right, honey." He looked down at her clothes still covered in blood. He took the cloth and wiped off the spots she had missed. "Do you want to grab some clothes, and I'll take you back to my place to clean up?"

Abby smiled. "That sounds wonderful. Then I want to go the hospital."

Paine scowled. "Why?"

"I want to check on Jeff."

"Why?"

Abby sighed. "I stabbed him, Paine. I need to make sure he's going to be okay."

"He tried to kill you, Abby. You don't owe him anything!"

She took his hand. "I know. I have to do this, Paine, and I'm hoping you'll go with me."

It was Paine's turn to sigh. "I'm going, Abby. I don't think I can let you out of my sight just yet."

Abby reached up and kissed him on the cheek. "Everything will be okay, now."

I hope so, Paine thought.

* * *

Abby turned in her chair again to try to find a more comfortable position. They had been there for hours, and she'd just about had enough. Her sore muscles were starting to complain again. Paine and Bill were still questioning Jeff, but she wasn't alone. Paine had made sure an officer stayed with her.

Abby was just about to get up and get her tenth cup of coffee when Paine walked in. He nodded at the officer, who left without saying anything. She stood up and went to Paine. He bent down and kissed her gently on the mouth. "How're you holding up?"

"Do you know who he hired to kill me?" she asked nervously.

"Let's take a seat, Abby, and I'll try to explain." Paine tried to steer her toward a chair.

Abby didn't budge. "I can't sit anymore. Just tell me what's going on."

Paine sighed. "Jeff doesn't know his real name. Just that he goes by the name the Black Angel."

Abby ran the name over in her head. "The Black Angel?"

"He only kills if he feels the person has done some kind of heinous act."

Abby nodded. "Jeff told him I was trying to kill his wife. He said he knew he'd been lied to when I helped Ben out of the wrecked car."

Paine nodded. "Jeff told us that part. The police have been looking for him for years. They know he's responsible for several murders but could never find him."

Abby frowned. "How do they know it was him, then?"

"Because the police figured out who would hire him."

Abby shook her head. "I don't understand."

Paine sighed. "I'm not explaining this very well." He turned back her. "The people whom he killed were either men who cheated on their wives or vice versa, and he was hired by the spouse. A lawyer had his coworker killed because he made partner before he did. He told the Black Angel that his coworker had cheated on the bar and didn't deserve it. There was one case in which a woman hired him to kill her daughter-in-law."

"Why?" Abby asked.

"Because she was wealthy, and her son had just died, and she didn't think her grandchild should be raised by the daughter-in-law, who was an alcoholic." Paine shook his head. "So in this guy's warped mind, he thought he was getting justice for these people who hired him."

"That's insane."

Paine agreed. "It was the police who actually named him the Black Angel or Angel of Death. The men and women who hired him could never ID him. They never met face-to-face with him. They would make a cash deposit into an account he would give them. Within minutes, the money was gone and the account closed."

"So we'll probably never know who he is, then," Abby murmured.

"Could you give a description of him?"

Abby shook her head. "No. His face was covered with black makeup, and it was dark."

Paine put his arm around her. Abby leaned back, resting her head on his shoulder.

"The police even tried to hire him using the website they were given," he said, "but he always seemed to know when it was a setup." Paine sighed. "The police will keep at it, Abby." He kissed the top of her head. "In the meantime—" He started when they heard a commotion in the hallway.

Abby groaned when she realized who was out there.

"Where is my husband?" Ashley demanded.

She heard somebody trying to calm her down, but Ashley wasn't hearing him. "I want to see my husband right now, and you have no right to stop me."

Paine stood as soon as he heard Ashley and went to the door. "Actually, he does." He stepped out into the hallway.

Abby followed him. She could see Ashley glaring at Paine. Then she turned her hate-filled eyes to her. Abby tried not to flinch when Ashley started for her; an ugly mask covered her face.

"You! This is all your fault."

Before Paine or Abby knew what was happening, she had slapped Abby across the face.

Abby cried out and put her hand to her face. She could feel the warmth from the slap.

Paine grabbed Ashley's arms and put them behind her back and started putting handcuffs on her.

"Let go of me, right now!" she yelled.

"I don't think so, lady," Paine said through clenched teeth.

"I didn't do anything wrong."

"I'm arresting you for assault." Paine looked at Abby. "Are you okay?"

She nodded. "Please, Paine. Just let her go."

Paine frowned at her. "Abby, I can arrest her for assaulting you."

Abby put her hand on Paine's arm. "Let her go," she said quietly.

Paine looked at her for a long time and then took the cuffs off Ashley. He watched her to make sure she didn't go after Abby again.

Ashley was rubbing her wrists looking at her. "I knew there was something going on between you two," she said nastily.

"There was nothing going on between us, Ashley." Abby tried not to scream in frustration.

Ashley snickered. "Right. I could see the way he looked at you."

Abby looked around and could see that several people had stopped to watch the show that was going on in front of them. She wanted to crawl into a hole and never come out again, but she knew that wouldn't solve anything.

She took a deep breath. "Ashley, I'm only going to say this one more time. There was never anything going on with me and Jeff." She took a step closer to Ashley. "Your husband tried to have me killed. When that didn't work out, he came for me himself. I've had a really bad night, and if you don't get out of my face right now, I swear I'll have Paine arrest you again," Abby said, her heart pounding in her chest. She looked at Paine and smiled. He smiled back.

Abby gave Ashley one last look, turned, and left. She had no idea where she was going, but she knew if she didn't leave, she would probably be the one arrested for assault. She decided to head for the cafeteria and wait for Paine there. Abby didn't complain when the same officer from before started to follow her.

She had just sat down with her second juice—she didn't think she could stomach another coffee—when Paine walked in. He sat down across from her. "We let Ashley see Jeff."

Abby nodded.

"Jeff told her everything."

Abby nodded again, not looking at him.

"Abby, honey, are you okay?"

"I think I'm going to have to move."

Paine chuckled. "I don't think that will be necessary."

Abby looked up at him.

"Ashley told Jeff she was selling everything and moving to her sister's in California. She told him he made this mess himself, so now he could take care of it himself."

Abby nodded and shrugged. "I can't say I blame her."

Paine scooted his chair closer to her. "When things have settled, I think we need to have a talk."

Abby looked at him. "What do you mean?"

"We'll wait until later, Abby. You're tired and need some rest."

Abby shook her head and bit her lip. "Oh no you don't. You're not going to say something like that and then tell me to wait until later."

Paine cleared his throat. "I'm just wondering— where do we go from here?"

Abby's heart started to pound in her chest again. She didn't know what to say. *That's not true, Abby. You do know what you want to say, but you're just too afraid to say it.* She wanted to be with Paine. She loved him and wanted to be with him always. *How hard could that be to say?* Abby tried to speak, but she wasn't able to form the words.

"Are you still thinking that what we feel for each other is a hero-worship thing?" Paine asked.

Abby looked at him and smiled. "No, I don't."

Paine smiled, too. "So do you think we should see where this goes? Go out on some dates? Maybe go dancing?"

Abby reached over and put her arms around Paine's neck. "I would love to go out on a date with you." She turned her head to look at the officer, who was trying to look anywhere except at them. "Are we going to take my bodyguard with us?"

Paine looked at the man and frowned. "I'm scared, Abby." He turned back to look at her. "How do we know for sure that the Black Angel is not going to come back for you?"

Abby thought about it for a minute. "Because, Paine, as crazy as this sounds, I think he's a man of his word."

Paine started to protest, but Abby stopped him. "He could have killed me tonight, but he didn't. He was angry that Jeff had lied to him. He was there tonight for Jeff. Not me." She went on when Paine didn't say anything. "You said it yourself. He only kills people who deserve it."

"It doesn't make it right, Abby."

"I'm not saying it does." She leaned away from Paine. "What I'm trying to tell you is that I'm not afraid. I feel safe. I *know* he won't be back."

Paine looked at her. "You damn well better be right." His voice was shaking. "I plan for us to be together for a long time."

Abby smiled. "Okay, bossy."

EPILOGUE

Six Months Later

They were all sitting in the backyard of Abby's house. School had just ended for Abby, and they were having a celebratory BBQ. Paine was at the grill, tending to the hamburgers.

For the first few weeks, Paine had barely left her side. Abby had tried to be patient, because she knew he was worried about her, but after the third week she couldn't take it anymore. She had been getting a project ready for her class, and he had been hovering. Again! "Paine, you need to go. Now!"

He had just looked at her.

"Did you hear what I said?"

"Are you trying to get rid of me?"

"Yes!"

His face had turned white. "You mean like forever?"

Abby had rushed over to him. "No. I don't mean forever." She had kissed him, and he grabbed her and devoured her mouth.

When they had come up for air, he rested his forehead against hers. "Don't scare me like that, Abby."

"I'm sorry. It's not what I meant at all." She had put her hands on his hips. "I'm safe. You need to go and do your detecting and let me do my teaching." He had kissed her again and left, even though he was reluctant.

Each day after that, he seemed to be more comfortable leaving her alone.

Paine had been right about Ashley. She did move to California, and Jeff was in prison. Paine also figured out how the Black Angel tracked them through the woods. He found a tracking device in her shoe. Abby tried not to think about it too much, because it still gave her the creeps that he had come into her house to place it there. The Black Angel had kept his word. She hadn't seen or heard from him since that night.

Ben and Jake were sitting at the picnic table arguing about who of the two of them had had the worse date. "She laughed like a duck," Ben was saying. "Every time she laughed, I felt like I should get my shotgun out and take aim."

"That's nothing," Jake said. "Do you remember the girl who whistled when she talked?"

Ben laughed. "Yes, but you still asked her out."

Jake shook his head. "I thought it was a joke. When it didn't stop on our date, I knew I was in trouble."

Abby couldn't help smiling. She had grown to love them like brothers and decided the arguing was how they showed their respect for each other.

Despite Jake's protest, they did go to Wyoming for Thanksgiving. Abby had been nervous about meeting Kate because she knew that Paine and the others truly cared about her. As soon as Abby met her and Jack, she liked them immediately. They welcomed her into their home with open arms. One night Kate and Abby were alone in the kitchen. "I'm really glad I got some time to talk to you alone."

"Okay," Abby said nervously.

Kate started loading the dishwasher, not saying anything. Abby had no idea what Kate was going to say, and it made her even more nervous when Kate didn't come right out and say what was on her mind. After the dishwasher was loaded, she started telling Abby about the ranch and her life with Jack.

Abby knew this wasn't what Kate wanted to talk about, and she couldn't take it any longer. "Kate, why don't you just tell me what you want to say?"

Kate laughed. "I'm sorry, Abby. I'm just not quite sure how to begin."

Abby felt sick. She knew how much Kate meant to Paine, and she was afraid that Kate wasn't going to like her. "It's okay, Kate, just say it."

"I've never seen Paine happier," Kate said. "After his divorce, I thought he would grow old and be miserable." She laughed. "But now I see him with you, and it—" Kate stopped and covered her mouth with her hand. "I'm sorry. I'm making a mess of this." Abby watched as Kate took a deep breath. "Has Paine told you what happened to me a couple of years ago?"

Abby nodded. "He did. And I'm very sorry."

"I'm not bringing it up to make you feel sorry for me. Paine helped me through that time, and he's very important to me." She sniffled. "I'm just glad that he's found you, and he's happy."

Abby walked up to Kate and smiled. "He makes me happy, too, Kate. And as long as we're together, I'll always try to make him happy."

Abby was surprised when Kate hugged her. "I know you will." The rest of the weekend had flown by, and Abby was disappointed when it had been time to leave. She and Kate e-mailed regularly.

"He's going to burn those hamburgers," Bill said, bringing Abby back to the present. She smiled. She had even grown to love the quiet man sitting next to her.

"Should I tell him he's burning them?" Abby teased.

"You're the only one who could," he said dryly.

Abby laughed. Paine looked at her, smiling. "What's so funny?"

"Bill wanted me to tell you that you're burning the hamburgers."

Bill started sputtering, and Abby laughed harder.

Paine scowled at Bill. "Do you think you could do a better job?"

Bill stood and winked at Abby. "I know I could." He took the spatula from Paine and started flipping burgers.

Paine took the seat that Bill had just vacated and reached for her hand. "You ready for our vacation?"

Abby smiled. "I'm actually quite excited about it."

Paine laughed. "Yeah, me too. This time, though, we won't have some crazy man chasing us."

"Yes, that's always a bonus."

"I called George and told him we would come by sometime next week."

Abby smiled. "It will be nice to see them again. Maybe they'll let us stay in the room with all the roses."

Paine gave her a lopsided grin. "I don't think so, honey."

"Spoilsport," she joked.

Paine leaned toward Abby so only she could hear. "I have other plans for us, and they don't include staying in a room where we would have to be quiet."

Abby swallowed. "Okay."

* * *

The Black Angel watched the house from across the street. He had scouted the house earlier and knew that Abby and her cop friends were in the backyard. He also knew that the cop in charge was her lover and would take care of her. So he wasn't really sure why he was sitting here except that he felt obligated to check up on her. He had almost killed an innocent, and that wasn't his way. He might be a killer, but he still had codes that he lived by, and without codes, there was no honor. He had learned that the hard way, but he had never forgotten.

He was leaving on a job in a couple of days and could be gone for several months; he had wanted to make sure she was okay before he left. Some might find it ironic that he had tried to kill her, and now he was her protector. It was his restitution to her.

He gave a small smile when he heard laughter coming from the backyard. She was going to be fine. Besides, he'd be back. The Black Angel started the car, and with a last look at the house, he pulled away.

48880710R00142

Made in the USA
San Bernardino, CA
07 May 2017